MY HEART TO TOUCH

A MAXWELL FAMILY SAGA - BOOK ONE

S.B. ALEXANDER

RAVEN WING PUBLISHING

My Heart to Touch
A Maxwell Family Saga - Book One
Copyright © 2018 by S.B. Alexander
All rights reserved.
First Edition:
E-book ISBN-13: 978-1-7329767-0-2
Print ISBN-13: 978-1-7329767-1-9

Visit: http://sbalexander.com
Editor: Red Adept Editing
Cover Design by Hang Le

This is a work of fiction. Names, characters, places and incidents either are the product
of the author's imagination or are used fictitiously, and any resemblance to locales,
events, business establishments, or actual persons-living or dead-is entirely
coincidental.

Chapter 1

Quinn

K ensington High's basketball team carried Alex Baker's coffin from the hearse to his final resting place. The closer they came, the louder the sobs, sniffles, and wails.

The cemetery was packed to the gills with students, moms, dads, sisters, brothers, and everyone in the small town of Ashford, Massachusetts. I knew of Alex, but I didn't know him like his teammates, his family, or even his girlfriend did. She was standing next to Alex's mom, sobbing uncontrollably. Brianna Masters was the *it* girl in school: beautiful, popular, rich, and sometimes the biggest snob this side of the Mississippi. But stories about her were for another time.

The day was all about mourning our number-one basketball player. Alex was loved my many, hated by few, and he'd had a future so bright that everyone had wanted to be with him, including me if I were being honest. I'd had a silent crush on Alex, even though he was two years older than my sweet sixteen years of age. Yet age didn't matter. The age difference between my mom and dad was three years.

Despite all that, Alex had never noticed me in the girlfriend sense. He'd come from money. I came from a farm. I was shy, a trait I'd inherited from my mom. Alex had been anything but shy. When he'd walked into a room, he'd commanded it like a conductor leading an orchestra.

When I walked into a room, the popular kids whispered about me. I didn't own designer clothes or name-brand shoes. I didn't wear skirts or high heels or shorts that showed off my butt. I didn't wear low-cut shirts or tons of makeup either.

I was as plain Jane as a girl could get. I lived on a farm, where the uniform of the day was boots, jeans, and a T-shirt unless it was winter; then I traded my T-shirts for heavy sweaters and a parka. Baggy was my style. But I was considered one of the nerds in school for reasons besides my wardrobe. I had my nose in books while the popular girls had their noses up jocks' butts. I dared not get started on my name— Quinn Thompson.

Tessa Stevens, my archenemy, hated by me, loved by others, ran around the school singing, "Quinn, Quinn will never win. You'll never get the boy."

Grrr. I tried not to swear. As my momma would say, "Quinn, God doesn't like potty mouths."

Tell that to Tessa.

Father Thomas opened his Bible as the team set down the coffin. The shiny mahogany wood glinted beneath the sad gray sky. A snowflake fluttered down before splattering on top of Alex. I swore it was an angel, seeping into the casket to take him up to heaven.

I believed in God. I believed that everyone standing in the cemetery to mourn Alex had a purpose on earth. I was raised a good Catholic girl. I went to church every Sunday with my parents and two brothers. I worked hard on the farm and even harder at my schoolwork. I followed the Ten Commandments. But I couldn't promise myself or anyone that I wouldn't break the fifth commandment, "Thou shall not kill," if Tessa Stevens kept giving me the stink eye.

She stood on the other side of the casket with her inky-black hair tucked under a knitted hat. Her bright-red lips stuck out like a spot on Mimi's body. My cow was prettier than Tessa. Okay, I was getting a little out of control. It would be impolite of me to stick out my tongue at my nemesis. So I lifted my chin and smiled, something I rarely did in front of her. Lately, I'd mostly been crying, not around her but in the confines of my barn loft or bedroom.

She'd beaten me in every possible way. She'd gotten the boy. She'd gotten the ice-skating awards. She'd even taken my best friend, Celia, from me.

Witch was a name I only called Tessa in my head. I was silently screaming it at that moment because Celia was staring at me as though she wanted to do something to me. I wasn't sure what. Her expression was a cross between *I'm sorry* and *I hate you.*

"Ignore her," my oldest brother, Carter, said in my ear.

My brothers were protective, like the Secret Service was to the president. I loved them for it, but I could handle my own matters... most of the time. That timid and shy side of me got in the way on occasion.

But we weren't standing out in the freezing cold to hash out my problems. We were there to mourn a legend in his own right—the school's basketball star. People whispered at games that Alex was a god among players, a loving brother to his sister, a supportive son to his mom, who had cancer, and a devout community member, volunteering his time to the Big Brothers Big Sisters organization.

Father Thomas began. "As we stand here today to mourn Alex Baker, we're reminded just how precious life can be. Celebrate his life. Let us pray."

Hanging my head, I gazed at my mud-crusted boots. I did pray. I prayed for Alex, his family, who was in tears near Father Thomas, and I prayed that the man who killed Alex would seek help for his disease. The man had gotten behind the wheel with an alcohol level well beyond the legal limit.

Booze would never be found at my parents' house. If my brothers drank at their high school parties, I didn't know. I'd never gone to one, and whenever they got home, I was always in bed or in my room. Besides, they had a tendency to shield me from things.

"We don't want you to be tainted by all the crap that goes on at high school parties," Carter had said to me too many times too count.

3

It didn't bother me that they didn't want me to go to the same parties as them or any party, especially one attended by Tessa. I would rather cut off my legs than be bullied by her or any of her posse.

The crowd broke up, and I realized Father Thomas had finished his sermon. I guess he didn't need to say much since he'd already said plenty at the church. My brothers started for the car, when Celia came running over.

Her espresso-colored eyes were filled with tears. I suspected for Alex. "Quinn, can we talk?"

Liam ran his hands through his wavy light-brown hair, which was filled with snowflakes. "We should go." He regarded me before he set his gaze on Celia, then he stiffened. I imagined he was angry with her for ditching me.

I jutted out my chin at my brother. "I'll meet you and Carter at the car."

Celia stared at Liam, and the longer she did, the more I figuratively scratched my head at her perplexing look. It seemed as though there was some kind of silent exchange between them.

Carter dangled his keys. "Come on, bro. Quinn, don't take too long."

Carter, Liam, and I had slight variations in hair color, but our eye color was the same. Momma referred to our amber eyes as the color of pennies, coppery when our emotions took a turn for the worse, and golden when we were happy and smiling.

My brothers got swallowed up in the crowd as people filtered out of the cemetery. Car doors opened and closed. Some people stayed behind and chatted. Others sniffled as they lingered by the coffin.

Celia watched Liam and Carter leave as I studied my former best friend. Her shoulders were hunched around her ears as she nibbled on her bottom lip.

"Care to tell me what's going on?" I asked.

Bigger snowflakes fell to the earth.

"Celia," Tessa called. "You're t—" Whatever she was about to say was cut off by her mother, who jerked on her arm.

Some of the rich folks in town were weird people. In some ways, the adults had morals, and in other ways, they didn't. I knew Tessa's mom was a harridan. The informal way to say it was bitch, but I didn't like calling people that. I despised when someone referred to me that way. My brothers always teased that I was a walking and talking dictionary.

Regardless, Tessa's mom had a way of talking down to others, including my mom. Anytime Mrs. Stevens shopped at our farm store, she treated my mother as if Momma were her slave. But my mom, Hazel Thompson, was the epitome of a saint, always smiling and helpful no matter what attitude people brought into the store with them.

Celia rolled her eyes before wiping her Rudolph nose with a tissue. "I want to be friends again. I'm sorry for what I did. Can you forgive me?"

I pursed my lips. My former best friend since the second grade had ditched me for our enemy, Tessa Stevens, as if I were a piece of trash. At the start of school in early September, Celia had wanted to begin her sophomore year with a bang. She'd wanted to live her high school years trying everything and anything she could, no matter the consequences. So Tessa, who was on the cheerleading squad, had told Celia that if she dropped me as a friend, then Tessa would vote to have her on the squad.

What Tessa hadn't told Celia was that in order to make the squad, my best friend had to lower herself to name-calling, spreading rumors about me, and playing pranks on me in gym class.

Now Celia looked miserable, although her misery seemed to be linked to Liam.

"Is there anything going on between you and Liam?" I asked.

Her perfectly plucked eyebrows lifted super high. "Where did that come from?"

I shrugged as a snowflake melted on my nose. "Call it female intuition."

She wagged a finger between us. "Liam is probably mad at me for breaking off our friendship. If you don't want anything to do with me, I understand." She lowered her gaze to her shiny brown boots.

I could tell she was leaving something out about her and Liam. I also knew she was sincere about being friends again. But I wasn't about to trust her yet.

I pressed my lips together. "You didn't just do one thing, Celia. You spread a rumor that I was easy. If it weren't for Carter, the entire football team would've tried to get in my pants."

Carter was big, mean, and most students feared him. He'd garnered his reputation after Noah Talbert had stolen his bike in the seventh grade. Carter's retaliation was shaving Noah's head. But the rumors about Carter and what he'd done to Noah had morphed into Carter pulling a knife on Noah, which wasn't true.

I tucked my hands into my winter coat. "You did something far worse than telling lies about me. You violated your moral code. You lowered yourself to Tessa's level. We pinky promised and blood promised since the second grade, Celia, that we would never stoop to Tessa's level of witchy, easy, condescending, and have no regard for others' feelings. We're better than that. You're better than her."

Celia pushed her black-framed glasses up on her button nose. "I quit cheerleading. It's not what I thought it would be, and I can't stomach the way you look at me at a football game or in class. Please, Quinn."

"I'm not going to give you ultimatums like Tessa did." I wasn't one to hold grudges. "How can I trust you, though?"

"I'll do whatever you want," she said.

I wasn't about to boss her around like Tessa had. "Let's start slow. Do you want to help out at the farm store tomorrow? It's the weekend before Thanksgiving, and the store will be busy."

Holidays were frantic and energetic. We sold not only handmade items, but jams, jellies, eggs, and other crafty things along with Christmas trees, although it was a week too early for buying a Christmas tree.

She smiled as though a pile of bricks had been lifted off her small shoulders. "I'll be there."

"Quinn," Liam called. "We got to go. Momma's making lunch."

I gave Celia the time to be at the store on Saturday, then I hurried out of the cemetery. Momma didn't like when we were late for meals. Besides, I had to get a big order ready for my mom's bestie, Eleanor Maxwell.

Chapter 2

Maiken

I pulled our Suburban into what looked like a mansion out of the Hollywood hills, rich, opulent, and huge. My aunt Eleanor and uncle Martin's home was even bigger than I had imagined.

My mom reached over with her dainty hand and touched my cheek. "Thank you for driving the rest of the way. Your dad would be proud of how you've stepped up to take care of us."

Boom. My heart rammed against my sternum. Anytime she brought up my dad, I held back a bucket of tears. He'd been the best father a son could have. When he wasn't fighting for our country in Iraq, he'd spent all his time with his family. Sadly, his life had ended on a battle-field thousands of miles from home.

"Maiken," my nine-year-old sister, Charlotte, called. "They have a lake. I want to go swimming."

Everyone in the car laughed. The snow was falling hard, covering the landscape, even the windshield. I would bet the lake would be frozen soon if the twenty-degree temperature held steady.

Mom, who was in the passenger seat, turned to face our clan. I was the oldest of eight siblings. My dad had kept my mom pregnant for many years. He used to kid around with her that he wanted fifteen kids. He believed that children were the backbone of what a family was all about.

Mom moved a strand of her dark-blond hair away from her face.

"Listen up. Your aunt Eleanor and uncle Martin have invited us to stay with them until we can get on our feet. So I want you on your best behavior. Are we clear?" Mom sounded like the lieutenant colonel my dad had been in the army. As soon as my dad had left for deployment, she'd cracked the whip.

"Yes, ma'am," we all singsonged.

Dad's death was fresh and still stung hard. It'd only been two months since two military personnel had knocked on the door. As much as we had known the risks involved with Dad's job, it didn't make the words they'd delivered that day any easier.

As soon as my mom had opened the door, she knew Dad wouldn't be coming home. I had as well. I was the man in charge now. I had to do everything in my power to make sure our family unit was solid. I'd promised my dad that if anything ever happened to him, I would step up.

I couldn't say I was stoked about the move and leaving my friends and the basketball team back in Fort Bragg, North Carolina. But my dad had taught me that sometimes we had to leave the things we loved behind to make sure that family was taken care of. My mom had done a great job on her own of keeping all of us kids in line. More than ever, she needed me to be the son my father had raised.

When Uncle Martin had made the trip down for the military funeral, he'd made the offer to my mom.

"I always told my brother that if anything happened to him, I would be here for you and the kids," Uncle Martin had said. "We would love for you to consider staying with me and Eleanor until you can get on your feet. The boys are out of the house, and we have plenty of room."

The military had given my mom benefits, but not enough to support a family of nine.

"Mom," Maple said. "How come you didn't want to move to Georgia with Aunt Denise?" Maple, my eleven-year-old sister, who was sitting behind me, wanted to live by the ocean, which was where my mom's sister had a tiny home that wasn't big enough for all of us.

Mom set her brown gaze on Maple, who resembled Mom. Each of

them had dirty-blond hair and dusting of freckles around their noses. "Aunt Denise doesn't have the room for us. We're here, and this is only temporary until we can get on our feet."

"Well, I like it here already," Harlan, Jr., said. At seven years of age, Harlan was a tornado of energy. So I imagined the enormous property surrounding the house would make my brother happy. The boy loved nature, including bugs. He was fascinated with fireflies in particular.

Someone knocked on the snow-covered window.

I opened the door to find Uncle Martin standing tall like the former soldier he'd been. His graying honey-colored hair was starting to collect snow at a fast pace. "We'll get the bags later. For now, let's get everyone inside and by the fire."

We hardly had snow in Fort Bragg, but I was sure my brothers and sisters would love to play in it. That was all they'd talked about while driving up. The newscaster on the radio had been talking about some snowstorm moving into New England.

We piled out of the car, and I grabbed Harlan. Since we weren't exactly experts in snow, I carried him so he wouldn't fall on the slick driveway. My mom held onto Charlotte's hand while the rest of my siblings climbed onto the deck, and shuffled into a kitchen I'd only seen in movies. We'd lived in military housing, and while the home was nice, it wasn't extravagant like the one I was standing in.

Stainless-steel appliances sparkled, pots and pans hung down over the massive island, and cabinets galore filled the space.

Aunt Eleanor was stirring something on the stove that smelled out of this world.

I set Harlan on his feet, and he ran out of the kitchen through an arched doorway.

"Ethan," Mom said to my fifteen-year-old brother. "Go help Harlan. He probably needs to use the bathroom."

Ethan rolled his brown eyes as he trudged after my brother, not giving Mom any flack like he usually did. He'd been super quiet since

Dad's death. I was worried about him, but I was hoping the move would help him clear his head.

"We're so happy you decided to come," Aunt Eleanor said.

Aside from my dad's funeral, I had only seen my aunt one time when I'd been a tike. Apparently, she'd been in a mental-health facility after my cousin, Karen, died. Nevertheless, she looked exactly like Elizabeth Taylor.

In fact, she'd turned some heads during my dad's memorial service when she'd glided in like a Hollywood star, dressed in an expensive tailored dress. I only knew it was expensive because the ladies in the church had whispered as much.

"Kids," Uncle Martin piped in. "Let's head down to the family room. You can watch a movie while the men unload the car." He eyed me, Marcus, and my thirteen-year-old brother, Jasper.

"I'll help too." Emma, Ethan's twin, batted her big brown eyes at Uncle Martin.

"So will I," Maple added.

My mom smoothed two hands over her short hair. She had always complained that her hair was too long and too much trouble, so she'd cut five inches off one day. My dad had loved her new look. He'd teased her that it was easier to pepper kisses all over her neck, something he'd loved to do.

I hoped one day I would have a loving relationship with someone, like my parents had. But I was sixteen, and girls were not on my radar. Honestly, girls were a distraction.

My buddies would brag about their girlfriends and their first kiss or how breasts felt. I listened but didn't see the draw. Dad had always taught me to stay focused on what I wanted, and girls, dating, and kissing weren't high on that list. I wasn't gay, and I wasn't oblivious to pretty girls, but sports were more my thing, basketball in particular. Anything other than basketball and family was white noise.

My sister Emma had told me that girls in school thought I was to die for. "Come on, Maiken," she'd said. "You're a boy for Pete's sake. You got to go out on a date sometime."

I would when I was good and ready. In my mind, the high school girls who'd thrown themselves at me were forward, pushy, gossipy, too confident, and self-absorbed. Maybe I would change my tune someday, but right now I had bigger things to worry about like how to help my mom.

We unloaded the car and ate lunch. When the younger kids crashed on the huge couch in the family room, Uncle Martin showed Ethan and me to a large bedroom on the first floor. At first, I thought we were taking the master suite, but I learned that the room had been my cousin Kade's.

With six bedrooms in the house, everyone was divided up with enough room that we didn't feel crowded, one of the perks of a mansion.

I was unpacking my suitcase when Ethan plopped down on one of the twin beds and slumped his shoulders, wearing one of his sad expressions that had become the norm for him since Dad had passed.

I sat across from him on the other twin bed. "What's wrong?" I knew he wasn't that stoked about moving.

He lifted his head. "I want to go home. I want to see Hannah. I want to see my friends. I want Dad back."

I briefly closed my eyes. The one thing that had sucked the big one about Dad being in the military was moving constantly. The change hadn't affected my younger siblings as much as it had Jasper, Marcus, Emma, Ethan, and me, although Emma was looking forward to a new school, and Jasper was much like Harlan. He loved the open space and nature. So I was sure Jasper would be fine.

But the bigger issue wasn't missing friends as much as wishing our dad were alive.

I took in a huge breath, staving off the need to cry, something I'd only done when I was alone. I couldn't let my brothers and sisters or even my mom see me break down. My family needed me to be strong, but it was difficult to mask my emotions or to get the memory out of my head of the two military men who'd shown up at our door.

"Ma'am," one of them had said to my mom. "It is with great

sadness to tell you that your husband, Lieutenant Colonel Harlan Maxwell, was killed on a mission in Iraq."

"How?" had been my question.

"Roadside bomb," one of the men in dress blues had said.

Ethan's sniffling brought me back to the present. Tears were streaming down his face.

I joined him on his bed and wrapped my arm around him. "Dude, we'll get through this. Hey, maybe we can go to a Celtics game." Ethan loved basketball as much as I did, but he wasn't a Celtics fan, and neither was I. We both cheered for the San Antonio Spurs.

He clamored to his feet, not saying a word, then locked himself in the en suite bathroom.

I could push to console him, but like all of us in the family, he needed time. So I resumed unpacking and tried to keep my mind in the moment. We had a great place to live. My mom had said it was only temporary, but I wondered how long we would be there. My dad had always said that we should make the best of where we were. So that was my motto, or at least I hoped I could take that advice.

Chapter 3

Quinn

The farm store was bustling with customers loading up on the essentials like eggs, farm-fresh milk, and other goodies. We were busier than normal, not only because of the holiday, but because a nor'easter was on its way and about to dump more snow than it had the night before.

Momma stocked her table with jams while I unpacked a box of honey on a display next to her. She wiped her hands on her apron. "We'll need to order more of everything." She set her russet-colored gaze on me.

I squatted down to collect the packing slip that had fallen out of the box. "What about the eggs?" It wasn't as if we could make our chickens produce more eggs at the snap of a finger.

Momma laughed. "Gray's farm will help if we run into a pickle."

We had had to purchase more eggs last year during Easter when eggs were in high demand.

I rose with two jars of honey. "Momma, did Dad find any help yet?" We were hiring for the Christmas season, to help with our Christmas tree business in particular.

She plucked the last jar of jam from the box and set it on the table. "Not yet. Is the order ready for Eleanor Maxwell?"

I continued to stack jars of honey on the table. "Yes, ma'am." I'd made sure I had taken care of Mrs. Maxwell's order the previous night, and all our call-ahead orders for that matter. But since Momma and Eleanor were great friends, Momma wanted to take care of her bestie. I did too. Eleanor was one of the sweetest ladies aside from Momma and Granny.

Momma kissed me on my temple. "Thank you. Now are you going to ask Eleanor if you can use the lake this year?" She moved a strand of her dark-brown hair that had fallen out of her bun behind her ear.

I stopped in my tracks. "Are you asking if I'm going to pick up skating again?" *Wow!* We hadn't spoken about me strapping on my skates in well over a year. I'd put my heart and soul into ice-skating and competing up until the eighth grade. But then I didn't know if I'd grown out of the sport or if I'd just hated losing all the time to Tessa Stevens.

My mom pursed her cranberry-stained lips. "Quinn, you can't let someone like Tessa stop you from doing something you love. You still love the sport, right?"

Voices hummed around us as customers browsed.

I shrugged, even though I loved how free I felt on the ice. "Momma, I want to put all my effort into my studies. If I can make a run for valedictorian, then maybe I could get an academic scholarship to Duke University or the University of North Carolina." Those were my top two choices, mainly because Duke's school of medicine was ranked high in the country. If I put all my time into competing on the ice, then I wouldn't have time to add to my college résumé and application.

Not only that, ice-skating cost money, and we weren't rich like Tessa Stevens. Besides, college tuition was much more expensive than we could ever afford, which was why if I was going to skate, it would be just for fun.

Momma crossed her arms over her tan sweater, her expression taking on one that said *listen to me, or else I will ground you to your room*. She looked beautiful no matter if she was scolding me or if she was covered in mud from trying to help Dad corral a pig who had gotten out of the pen. Then she sighed; her features loosening. "I guess

I can't argue with that. School is important, and I know you want to be a doctor. I just want to be sure you're not letting Tessa get in your head. I know you, Quinn. You can study, make valedictorian, and skate. You don't have to give up one for the other."

That might have been true, but skating wouldn't support me for the rest of my life, although I did enjoy getting out in the cold weather and doing jumps like the triple toe and Salchow or even just gliding around the ice.

I pecked her on the cheek. "I love you. But if I do skate, it will be for fun."

Momma moved hair off my face. "You should be having fun in high school. These next three years should be all about growing and exploring, and dare I say boyfriend too. Please don't hide away like you did last year."

I rolled my eyes as I thought of how awful freshman year had been. The juniors and seniors had rolled out the red carpet when it came to bullying and teasing freshmen. One senior had said it was tradition. *Horse cocky.*

Sophomore year wasn't proving to be any better. The bullying hadn't diminished. Boys didn't see me as girlfriend material. Most only saw me as a nerd who could help them with their schoolwork. I wasn't interested in any of the boys in my grade. Plus, Celia had ditched me, although she had shown up to help at the store—a sign that she really did want to make amends.

I briefly considered Celia, who was working the register. "Momma, boys in my high school only think about sports and getting into a girl's pants." I delivered the last part in a hushed whisper. That was mostly true for the jocks, which was what we called the boys who wore letter jackets and played sports and thought they were above anyone else.

My mom didn't flinch. If I'd said all that to my dad, he would've turned dark red, gotten his shotgun out, and prepared to shoot the boy who dared to look at me. My brothers would've done the same. None of the boys in my school were good for me according to my oldest brother, Carter. If any boy stepped close to me when Carter was around, chaos ensued.

But he had nothing to worry about. I'd grown up with big brothers who had taught me how to handle myself. Even Momma had made sure I knew where to kick first if the opposite sex tried anything I didn't like.

The bell on the door dinged, announcing more customers. They trudged in, stomping their boots on the mat to rid them of the snow.

"The right boy will respect you. If they don't, you remember what I taught you?"

I smiled. "Yes, ma'am. Hit them where it counts."

Satisfied with my answer, she scurried off to help, of all people, Mrs. Stevens, Tessa's mom.

Celia bounced over.

I scanned the modest room, which had ten customers, but no one was ready to check out.

Celia flicked her ponytail over her shoulder. Her dark hair matched the color of her eyes, and she wore a ton of makeup, which was odd considering her mom wouldn't let her use the stuff. "Is everything okay?" She pointed at my mom. "You two were huddled like she was giving you a speech. Did you get in trouble?"

Mrs. Stevens, who was bundled up for the winter storm, nodded at something Momma had said.

I took off one of my fingerless gloves. "We were talking about boys. Nothing special." I wanted to trust Celia. I wanted to believe she was serious about being friends again. I did miss her, our talks, riding horses, and just playing on the farm.

She hooked her arm in mine. "Quinn, boys are everything. Don't you want to experience your first kiss or go out on your first date?" She sounded as though Tessa had filled her mind with dirty stuff. "I know I do."

Celia was pretty underneath the heavy blue eye shadow and rose blush. She could've probably had her pick of any guy. But in my opinion, she was wrong about boys. "Why would you say they're everything? Explain." I had to hear her view on the topic because I only saw jocks that were self-centered, rude, and belligerent. From the conversations I'd overheard in some of my classes, the jocks bragged about whatever sport was in season or their latest conquests. *And ew!* I didn't like what I'd heard on the topic of their sex lives either.

Celia guided me over to the doorway that led to the storage room and the bathroom. "Quinn, we're women. We have needs."

I busted out laughing. "Needs? Like in coitus?" That was the word we'd always used instead of sex.

She playfully punched me on the arm. "Come on. Don't you feel hot and tingly down there when you see a boy you like?"

I could feel my face turning red despite the fact that I didn't have my eye on anyone who gave me those feelings. "Who is he?" She was crushing on someone. I'd known her too long not to see the signs of red cheeks, red neck, and that faraway look in her eyes. The last time she'd displayed all those signs, she had the hots for Danny in the fifth grade.

She studied me. "Do you really want to know?"

"If you want to tell me." She'd better tell me, because we were friends, and friends told each other everything.

She glanced past me. "Don't get upset. But I have a crush on your brother Liam."

Now their silent interaction from the day before made sense. "So you lied to me yesterday? Something is going on between you two?" I didn't care that she had a crush on my brother or that my brother might like her. "If you want me to trust you, then you better start telling the truth."

She shuddered. "I kissed Liam. That's all. The tension you saw between us yesterday was more because he's afraid I'll kiss him again. I don't want to talk about it right now." She sounded heartbroken.

Again, I didn't care if they liked each other, but I did wonder if her sudden apology had had anything to do with Liam. "Celia, do you want to be friends again because you want to get close to Liam?" If she said yes, then I would kick her out right then.

Her mouth fell open. "No! I was honest when I said I miss us." She seemed sincere in her delivery.

The conversation was getting a little tense, and we had customers to attend to. "We can talk more later. But I will say this. Don't use me to get to Liam."

She pushed her glasses up on her nose. "I promise you on my grandmother's grave that I would never do that. I need to get back to the register. Your mom is eyeing me." She bounced off.

I believed her only because I knew how much she adored her grandmother, and Celia didn't throw out promises easily. Still, time would tell how our friendship would evolve.

I headed into the storeroom, thinking of what my mom had said about dating. I didn't get a chance to dwell on the topic before my mom came in. "Eleanor is here."

"I'll be right out with Mrs. Maxwell's order." I made quick work of organizing the box of eggs, jams, marmalade, and bacon. Eleanor always had a big order, but on that day, she'd ordered double of every-thing. She'd mentioned to Momma that she had family coming into town.

I collected the box and had just started to leave the storeroom when Celia flew in.

"O-M-G. You have got to see him." She practically dragged me out with her. I'd known Celia since the second grade, and I knew two things excited her—horses and Shawn Mendes. I didn't see a horse anywhere in the store, and there was no way Shawn Mendes would be in our small town in Massachusetts.

We settled in the doorway, looking out at the various customers milling around.

She leaned in. "He's over by the hats."

I followed her gaze, or more like her finger, which she had pointed at what Momma would call a tall drink of water.

"Isn't he dreamy?" Celia cooed.

The boy's sandy-blond hair was cut short on the sides like the men I'd seen in those military movies my dad loved to watch.

I wanted to ask her what had happened to her crush on Liam. Instead, I sighed like Celia had at the Shawn Mendes concert. The somewhat heavy box in my hand felt weightless.

Dreamy didn't begin to describe the boy at all. He had a strong jaw, a somewhat crooked nose as though he'd broken it in a fight, and a broad chest.

He tried on a beanie that my granny had made then examined himself in the small mirror we had on the counter for that very reason.

"I love how that Henley fits him," Celia said.

Dreamy Boy checked the price on the hat then returned it to the pile. My heart fell a notch. He was dressed nicely enough in jeans, army boots, and no jacket, which seemed odd considering the temperature was around fifteen degrees outside.

"You should go talk to him," Celia said without looking at me.

I didn't know if he'd heard Celia or if he felt us staring, but he lifted his head. When he did, I flinched and almost dropped the box.

Celia waved.

The blood drained from me. "Don't bring attention to us."

Granny had always said that one day, Celia would be trouble. I'd laughed many times when I'd heard that. But I was beginning to think that Granny had some foresight.

Regardless, I didn't need some boy to pick on me or look down at me as if I were beneath him, and Dreamy Boy was giving me that vibe until one side of his mouth turned up. Whether he was looking at Celia or me, one thing was certain—my pulse galloped as fast as my horse, Apple. I couldn't look away.

His big blue eyes sucked me in and gobbled me up. He had hair like James Dean—thick, sandy blond, and longer on top. His pretty lips were to die for. Yeah, I was crushing hard.

"He kind of looks like Zac Efron only with blond hair," Celia said.

He certainly had those belly-tingling blue eyes like Zac Efron.

"Quinn," Momma called a little too loudly. "Mrs. Maxwell needs her order."

The boy's eyes widened as though he knew Eleanor.

I shook off my trance, left Celia standing near the fridge full of raw milk, and hurried to the register.

Eleanor beamed at me as she retrieved her wallet. She was as beautiful as ever with a furry white hat that covered her black hair.

I set the box down, and the boy swaggered up to Eleanor. I would've guessed him to be either my age or one year older.

He studied me, appearing to want to eat me. *Figures.* When boys looked at me, they usually had one thing on their minds, especially when their eyes dragged down to my breasts. At sixteen, I was a little larger in that area than the other girls in my grade, even Celia.

I could feel my lips curling into a snarl.

Eleanor handed me her credit card. "Quinn, the lake should freeze soon if the cold temps stay like they are. Any plans to skate?"

I shrugged. "I don't know yet."

She touched Dreamy Boy's arm. "My nephew, Maiken, and his siblings would probably love to learn how to ice-skate."

Maiken? I rolled that name around in my head a few times. Odd name, but cool as well.

Maiken gave his aunt a funny look.

Celia finally ran up. "Hi, I'm Celia," she said to Maiken.

He nodded, not saying a word.

"So are you new in town?" Celia asked.

I rang up the bill, waiting for him to answer, but he collected the box and left.

Eleanor sighed. "Sorry about Maiken. You'll have a chance to talk to him again at school. He'll be attending Kensington High."

Celia squealed.

I gave Eleanor a fake smile.

When she was gone, I sighed so heavily, I blew hair from my face. I had mixed emotions about the mysterious Maiken Maxwell. I liked his looks. I didn't like his impolite attitude.

Chapter 4

Maiken

Sitting on my new twin bed, which felt foreign to me, I gripped the framed photo of my dad as if I were holding on to the ledge of a cliff six thousand miles above a canyon. A tear slipped out and hung on my bottom eyelid. Dad would never cheer from the stands at any of my basketball games or shout at me to shoot that three-pointer or block my opponent. He would never see me grow into a man or witness my marriage or play with my children like grandfathers did.

I was trying not to get depressed or mourn too much. Dad had always taught me to be strong no matter the consequences. I found it difficult to even breathe sometimes, though.

Mom kept telling my siblings and me that Dad was watching us from heaven so we had to be on our best behavior. Harlan, the youngest, would look up at the sky and say hi to Dad. Then he would proceed to let Dad know he wasn't getting into trouble. That had always gotten a chuckle out of everyone.

"So, Dad," I said to the picture of him kneeling next to his military unit's German shepherd, Desert, who was a bomb-sniffing dog. "We moved. We're at Uncle Martin's house. Nice digs too. We're doing okay. We all miss you terribly. I know Mom is hurting badly inside. I hear her whimper at night in her room. But you know she's tough as nails. At least she shows us how strong she is on the outside." Another tear fell and slid easily down my cheek.

Knuckles rapped on the door before it squeaked open. "Maiken, can I come in?"

I wiped away the tears as fast as I could before I tossed a look over my shoulder. My cousin Kade lingered in the doorway, wearing a blank expression.

I set Dad's picture next to me on the bed. "It's your room." I sounded harsh as I sniffled.

Padding across the carpeted floor, Kade leaned against the window's ledge, scanning the freshly painted room. "I miss this bedroom. Lots of memories in here." He stabbed a finger toward me. "Is that a picture of your dad?"

I was reluctant to show him. I felt as if I were handing Kade my heart. Nevertheless, I handed him the photo because his tone was soft and sincere.

He flicked his gaze at me then my dad. "You look just like him." My cousin's strong features turned sour. "It's sad that we haven't been closer to your family. When we left Texas, life changed drastically for us. That was..." He paused. "Let's see, I'm twenty-four now. So nine years ago."

I'd overheard my parents talking one night about how my cousin Karen had been accidentally shot by her best friend at the age of twelve. I couldn't imagine what the family had gone through. I wouldn't or couldn't deal if anything like that happened to any of my brothers or sisters. Then again, the only one in our family who owned a gun had been my dad, and his gun was military issue, which meant he didn't bring it home with him.

I couldn't think of anything to say except, "Well, we're here now." My tone had lost its previous harshness.

Kade and I were family. Yet I felt as if I were sitting across from a stranger. His life had changed back then, and ours had changed too. Military life had dictated how we lived, where we lived, and when we moved. So it hadn't always been easy to visit family.

He handed the picture back to me. "My mom tells me you helped her at Thompson's farm store yesterday. I wanted to thank you."

When Aunt Eleanor had mentioned she was heading to pick up some groceries at the local farm, I'd jumped at the chance to get out of the house. Even though we were staying in a mansion, the house felt suffocating to me. Not only that, Uncle Martin had asked if I could help Aunt Eleanor while he and my mom discussed some military paperwork.

I lifted a shoulder. "It was no biggie. So you work at a nightclub in town?" Aunt Eleanor had told me all about my cousins and what they did for a living. "Do you need some help?"

Kade grinned. "You want to work? What about school? I understand that you're a great basketball player. Are you going to try out for the high school team?"

He sounded as if it were a sin to work while going to school. I didn't want to think that my family was a bunch of snobs, but the thought had crossed my mind, especially considering Kade was looking at me as if I'd grown two heads.

I jutted out my chin. "If we're going to be here for a while, then I want to earn my keep."

His grin didn't fade. "And school?" He was starting to sound like my dad, and while that wasn't a bad thing, I didn't need him to step into my father's shoes.

I pressed my lips together. "Didn't you have a part-time job when you were in high school?"

He crossed his arms over his chest. "I didn't. I had to take care of my brothers and my mom, especially when my dad was on deployment. I'm not trying to play your father."

I narrowed my eyes. "Then don't."

He raised his hands. "All I'm trying to say is I've been in your shoes, Maiken. When Karen died, it was the hardest thing I had to go through. When my mom had to get help for her depression, that was extremely hard as well." His tone was even and calm, but so much sadness washed over him.

I shuddered and sighed at the same time, realizing I was being a jerk.

He dragged a hand through his brown hair while lowering the other one. "I would like to help, not as your dad but as a friend. Lacey and I are living at her old man's house in town while our house gets built. But I'm here if you need someone to talk to." He pushed off the windowsill, waving me over. "I want to show you something."

I joined him, and we gazed out at the snow-covered landscape.

Kade tucked one hand in his jeans pocket while he pointed a finger. "You see that clearing to the north?"

Off to my right, a cluster of trees surrounded an opening as though someone had cut a swath through the woods.

"That's where we're building our house." He beamed with pride, love, and so much more. "I know you can't see much right now because of the snow, and the contractor hasn't gotten the entire frame built yet. But on a clear day, you'll be able to see the roof of our house from here."

I didn't know why he was sharing all this with me. Maybe it was his way of telling me that life will get better. But I couldn't envision anything past the moment. Silence bounced between us as we watched the snow fall. I could use a friend. After all, Kade knew what it was like to lose someone, and he seemed happy.

"I don't know if I'll play basketball," I said. "I want to, but I don't know how long we'll be here." I didn't want to get in a groove with the team only to let them down. I'd done that enough times in the past because of my dad's military orders, and it sucked to say goodbye or leave before the team went to the playoffs. Besides, a job was more important at the moment. "I need to help my mom anyway."

"I guess you haven't heard."

I gave him a sidelong glance, looking him in the eye since we were the same height. "You're building us a house?" Sarcasm laced my words.

One side of his mouth turned upward. "My parents are leaving after the holidays for a month-long cruise. So your family will have the house all to yourselves. But I'll be close by in case your mom needs help. Lacey has offered to help with the kids as well."

I wanted to shout that we didn't need help, but if I got a job, then my mom would need some assistance, although my older siblings helped take care of the younger ones.

As though Kade were in my head, he said, "If you're looking for a job at least through the holidays, my mom said Thompson's farm is hiring. They sell Christmas trees."

I did recall seeing a sign taped to the entrance when I'd been there the day before. But I'd thought they wanted to hire someone to work in the store, and after those two girls had stared at me as though they wanted to strip me naked, I'd decided no way. They'd reminded me too much of the girls in my last high school—pushy and aggressive.

My buddy Xavier had said I was a moron for not capitalizing on a good thing—pretty girls, virgins, and I could have my pick of the litter.

Forward girls weren't my thing. Girls who wanted to be seen with a hot guy weren't my thing. Girls who wanted to boss me around definitely were not my thing.

Dad had always taught me to respect girls. He'd said I should treat a girl as if she were a Hollywood star—roll out the red carpet, and above all else, make sure she knew I was only looking at her. Dad had said the minute my eyes strayed was the minute I would lose her respect, then she would think I was like the boys who only wanted to get her into bed.

Kade waved a hand in front of me. "Maiken, are you in there?"

I chuckled. "I don't think working on a farm is for me."

"A job is a job," Kade said. "Besides, Quinn is your age. She's also pretty."

I could feel my eyebrows coming together. "Where did that last part come from?" I got the impression he was trying to play matchmaker. Still, he wasn't wrong. Quinn was eye-catching with big brown eyes and hair that fell to her waist.

"My mom mentioned the way you and Quinn looked at each other. That's all."

Funny.

Aunt Eleanor thought I'd been rude to Quinn. She'd counseled me in the car on the way home that I could've been more polite. I might've been if that girl, Celia, hadn't rubbed me the wrong way. I could feel her staring at me while I'd been trying on hats. Actually, I could feel both Celia and Quinn ogling. I was beginning to understand what Emma had said about girls thinking I was to die for.

Girls weren't on my agenda. So it was time to move on to another topic. "What about helping you at the club?"

The nor'easter was in full force. The longer we looked out the window, the harder the snow fell.

My cousin rested his hand on my upper back. "Tell you what. Once you get situated in school and get into a routine around here, then we can chat. The club is slow anyway right now."

I could do that. What I wouldn't do was apply for a job at the Thompson farm. I didn't see myself working on a farm. Besides, I wanted something steady, not a job that would end after Christmas. I also didn't want to be subjected to Quinn and her friend drooling over me. Creepy was a term that came to mind, and I didn't do creepy.

Chapter 5

Quinn

The halls at school bustled with students milling around and dragging themselves to their lockers or into classrooms. I was one of those kids. We'd been out of school for a week between the snowstorm and the Thanksgiving holiday. The farm had been overly busy with people buying Christmas trees. We hadn't found anyone to help yet. Dad thought that the two feet of snow we'd had was the main reason no one had applied for the job.

The mood among the students seemed cheerier than before Alex's funeral. Maybe the time off had helped everyone to heal a little more.

I leaned against my locker while Celia opened hers. "Do you think we'll see Maiken today?" she asked.

I couldn't deny that I'd been thinking about the new boy since I had laid eyes on him at the farm store exactly nine days ago. Part of why he was on my mind had something to do with the conversations Celia and I had had about boys and feelings and dating. In fact, it had been wonderful to rekindle our friendship.

She'd even spilled about what had happened between her and Liam. Apparently, she'd forced herself on him and kissed him. My brother hadn't reciprocated. Instead, he'd walked away. He hadn't spoken to her since, and if she had been at my house or working in the store when Liam had come in, he'd been nice with a quick hi, but he hadn't hung around.

"May I remind you that you like my brother?"

She closed her locker, clutching her algebra book against her chest. "I told you he doesn't want me. He still thinks I'm a little girl, running around the farm, screaming because one of the pigs is chasing me."

I couldn't help but snicker. That had been a funny day when one of the pigs had gotten out of the pen and made a beeline for Celia as she'd walked to the barn.

"Hush," she snapped. "Liam probably thinks I'm prim and proper or one of those bitchy girls like Tessa. Maybe that's the reason he doesn't want anything to do with me."

I arched a brow. "Or maybe he's mad you ditched me like I was some kind of open wrapper." Celia had never been like Tessa until Tessa had infused my BFF with some type of witch juice that had changed Celia into someone I didn't know.

The voices in the hall lowered to a hum before it got quiet. At first, I thought everyone was listening to us, which wouldn't have been all that surprising. Lots of kids in school had elephant ears. Elephants didn't exactly have superior hearing, but they could hear sounds humans couldn't.

Celia and I both scanned the hall, and as if the sea had parted, everyone moved, opening up a swath. A boy with a wavy crop of brown hair swaggered toward us alongside a beautiful girl who looked exactly like him, only her wavy locks were long like mine, down to her buttocks. She whispered something to the boy, and when his lips parted into a smile, some of the girls in the hall sucked in a sharp breath.

They both stopped at a locker outside the math classroom. Then the girl waved. "Hi, everyone. I know you're curious about the newbies, so let me put you at ease." She stabbed a pink fingernail at her companion. "This is my brother Ethan. I'm Emma, and yes, we're twins. We're freshmen. Any questions?"

Ethan chuckled as he fiddled with his locker, glancing at the small white paper in his hands.

Tessa Stevens bobbed out of the crowd, dressed in thigh-high black boots over black leggings, and a cable-knit red sweater that brought out her inky-black hair. Even though we were enemies, I still thought she was one of the prettiest girls in school—thin, curvy, with skin free of pimples. Granted, most kids tried to conceal their pimples. I was one of them. But for as long as I'd known Tessa, she'd never had a pimple.

Tessa put one foot forward and placed a hand on her hip. "Freshmen don't belong in this wing of the school." She sounded horrified.

Whispers peppered around.

Most girls ran from Tessa or cowered.

Emma got in Tessa's face. "Tell that to the principal."

The crowd was so riveted on the potential catfight until a voice, deep and commanding, said, "Emma."

Celia gripped my arm as if she were having a heart attack. "It's him. It's Maiken."

It took me a moment to register her words as my gaze swung to the boy sauntering down the hall with a sense of purpose. Maiken Maxwell exuded confidence, commanding the attention of the students without saying anything but Emma's name.

Emma didn't back down from Tessa. Tessa, however, did turn to see who had interrupted her potential *I'm queen of this school* speech. The moment Tessa laid eyes on Maiken, she wiggled her hips toward him.

Emma started talking to Ethan. They both laughed as if to say, "hey, everyone, watch this."

I couldn't look away, because the moment Tessa touched Maiken might be the moment I stood up to her once and for all.

Tessa held out her hand to the sandy-blond hunk with the bluest eyes on the planet. "Hi, I'm Tessa. And you are?"

Celia huffed. "There went our chances."

"You know he's probably like every other guy in this school who wants one thing," I said under my breath.

Celia didn't take her attention off of Tessa. "Who cares if he wants sex?"

I wanted to say I did. Instead, I kept my mouth shut. I didn't want to argue with Celia about how girls should carry themselves around boys and not be so easy or forward like she'd been with Liam.

Emma pushed her way in between Tessa and Maiken. "He's my brother, and I would highly suggest you keep your claws off him."

Tessa snarled.

The warning bell rang. That was my cue to duck out of the crowd. The last thing I wanted was to bring attention to myself, and I could do that easily if Tessa noticed me. She would do something to embarrass me in front of Maiken, and I wasn't as bold as Emma. I couldn't tell Tessa to stick it where the sun didn't shine.

Momma had taught me to mind my manners and ignore comments and rumors that were directed at me. "Be better than Tessa. She wants you to fight back. So don't give into her." Momma's advice was hard to adhere to. Sometimes I had to hold back tears or my fists or the urge to run and hide.

I hiked my backpack over my shoulder. "I'll meet you in class," I said to Celia. Then I made my way around students who were going to their first-period class like me.

As I approached my classroom, which was close to where Tessa and Maiken were standing, Maiken swung his gaze toward me.

Tessa turned. Then as if the world wanted to make my life miserable, Tessa sized me up and opened her mouth. "Quinn, you're looking rather ratty today." Her sweet voice felt like acid burning my skin. "Did you step in pig shit before coming to school?"

Maiken had a blank expression as he considered me, much like he'd had when he was at the store. Regardless, my face had to be as red as a ripe homegrown tomato. I didn't dress in designer clothes like Tessa. I didn't own fancy leather boots. My boots were made for working. But I wasn't wearing my work boots. I had on nice suede boots that I'd gotten for Christmas the previous year. They had fur around the edges, a zipper on the sides, and covered my calves almost up to my knees. Momma called them practical. Sure, I had some dirt on my jeans from when I'd brushed against Apple's stall that morning, but I certainly didn't look ratty.

Celia came up behind me. "Shut up, Tessa."

Maybe Celia's friendship was worth saving after all, although she would get mad at me for not telling Tessa off.

"Why fuel her fire?" I'd always said to Celia.

Maybe I would give Tessa a taste of her own medicine. Everyone had a breaking point. Tessa just hadn't found mine yet. Actually, I didn't know what would send me over the edge and make me finally put Tessa in her place.

Emma bumped Tessa with her shoulder before she came up to me. "Don't let her rattle your cage. You're beautiful."

Now I was even redder.

Celia sneered at Tessa, who narrowed her dark-as-night eyes before she flipped her hair over her shoulder, poked out her small breasts, and pushed them into Maiken's arm.

He didn't move or give any indication that he was happy with the way Tessa was acting. Ethan sure was, though, which was evident by his shocked expression. Then Maiken lowered his gaze to Tessa and smiled. He actually smiled at her. He couldn't be cordial and nice when Mrs. Maxwell had introduced us. Instead, he'd fixated on my chest before he'd stormed out of the store. But he could chummy up to Tessa.

Suddenly, my stomach was ready to lose the bagel I'd eaten for breakfast.

"My brother is just being nice," Emma said at my side as though she knew what I was thinking.

Despite my irritation, my body was tingly. I would bet every girl in school would be drooling at Maiken's feet. He had an aura about him like Alex had had—tough, quiet in some ways, and vocal in others. In the looks department, though, Maiken had Alex beat by a long shot, at least in my eyes.

I was digging Maiken's bad-boy persona, including his unlaced army boots instead of the Chucks Alex had always worn. I preferred Maiken's blue eyes, which reminded me of the deepest part of the ocean, instead of Alex's green orbs. Above all else, Maiken's hair was thick on top, shaven on the sides, and a few strands flopped over his forehead.

Sigh!

Regardless of their differences, one thing was certain. Whether Maiken was being nice or not, I had no chance with him.

Chapter 6

Maiken

I navigated the empty halls of the school on my way to the gymnasium. Coach Dean wanted to chat with me. I imagined about basketball. Quiet conversations around school that day had surrounded a student who had died in a car accident recently. Apparently, he'd been a senior and a star basketball player.

Once inside the sports complex, I took a sharp right, headed down the hall, through the double doors, and into the gym. The basketball team was running suicides, their sneakers squeaking on the wood floor.

The cheerleaders were huddled at the far end of the gym, talking.

I threaded my fingers through my hair as I wound my way around the perimeter, skirting in front of the bleachers until I was standing next to an average-height bald man with a whistle hanging around his neck. I assumed he was Coach Dean.

He blew his whistle. "Take five."

The team stopped. Some bent over, breathing heavily, while others darted for their water bottles. The cheerleaders glanced toward me, but I couldn't tell whether their attention was on the team or me.

Nevertheless, by the time the last bell of the day had chimed, I'd wanted to pull out every strand of my hair. Girls in the halls, in class, and in the cafeteria had stared at me as if I were part of a buffet line. Maybe I was hyperaware of the opposite sex now that Emma had not so politely thrown out, "I told you so," when I'd seen her during lunch.

I held out the note I'd gotten from the admin office. "Coach Dean, you wanted to see me."

He took the note. "You must be Maiken Maxwell. Thank you for showing up. I hear you're quite the basketball player. Or I should say I read your file. Is it your plan to play for Kensington?"

I regarded Coach, who was almost a head shorter than me. "With all due respect, I'm not stepping into a dead person's shoes." I didn't need the headache or attention or comparison. "Aren't tryouts over with?" Every high school had tryouts that time of year with the first game usually starting in early December. If I were going to play, then I had to at least try out. Otherwise, it wouldn't have been fair to those who had and didn't make the team.

"I guess you heard, then. Alex was a great player." Coach glanced up at the ceiling then blessed himself with the sign of the cross. "But you wouldn't be stepping into his shoes. I read that you're a shooting guard."

"Are you looking for a shooting guard?"

Coach Dean looked out at the center court at the same time a boy as tall as me walked up with a basketball underneath his arm. His hair was sweaty, and his pimples glowed as he snarled at me. "Coach, we have others in this school who want to play. The new boy doesn't belong on our team."

It was my turn to snarl, and the words *piss off* were on the tip of my tongue. If anything got my temper going, it was assholes like this kid who felt threatened by a newcomer. I'd dealt with plenty of people like that while moving from school to school. I should have been immune to guys like him, but I wasn't in the mood. I certainly wasn't going to stand there and let him throw barbs at me.

Coach crossed his bulky arms over his Kensington High golf shirt. "Chase, I'm the coach of this team, and you don't have a say in who plays or doesn't."

Chase narrowed his dirt-colored eyes at Coach. Then he turned on his heel and went back to the team. All but one guy started whispering. The lone ranger seemed familiar to me, but I couldn't place the dude.

Coach addressed me. "If you want to play, be here tomorrow to practice with the team and show us what you can do." Then he trotted to center court, where he gathered the team.

Chase cornered him and started to open his mouth, but Coach raised his hand. If I played, Chase would be a problem, and I didn't need problems. *You're not a shoo-in yet. You have to show Coach what you got.*

I was about to leave when Tessa Stevens bounced up, bubbly and licking her lips. "Maiken," she said in a sweet voice.

I knew better than to think she was sweet. I'd gotten a glimpse of how she had interacted with Emma in the hall before school. She was the type of girl I didn't pay much attention to—crass, snappy, and bitchy. More than that, I despised the way Tessa had bullied Quinn that morning. I'd wanted to shout at Quinn to stand up for herself, but I hadn't wanted to bring more attention to her. It had been evident by the way she'd cowered that she'd wanted to hide.

Tessa flipped her ponytail over her shoulder. "Some of us are going over to Shaker's, a new burger-and-shake place in town. Do you want to join us?"

The need to pull out my hair increased tenfold. *Be polite. Be a gentleman.* "I can't." I pivoted on my heel.

In a flash, she was in front of me. "Did I do something to make you mad?" She pouted, and her dark eyes became pinpricks.

"I need to help my mom. Sorry." I hurried out of the gym as if a bear were chasing me.

Before I knew what was happening, something hard slammed into my chest. I barely had time to grip the sides of the girl's arms to catch her from falling.

Once she was steady, she clasped a hand over her nose. "Ow." Tears floated in her amber eyes.

It took me a second to orient my vision, and when I did, I was looking at the girl with butterscotch hair who suddenly made my stomach flutter. "Quinn, right?" I knew who she was, but her sweet-scented shampoo was making my brain turn into a pile of mush.

She nodded as she sank her teeth into her bottom lip, an act that seemed to do something to my insides in a good way.

Holy cow! A girl had never caused me to get all giddy.

"Sorry," I said. "Can I see your nose?" As hard as we'd collided, I suspected she would have a black eye or two.

When she dropped her tiny hand, I noticed a smattering of freckles around her small nose. But the freckles weren't what had me touching her nose or had my finger traveling up toward her eyes. She had the thickest lashes I'd ever seen on a girl. Then again, I hadn't been physically close to many girls other than my sisters, and maybe Sarah in the fourth grade. She'd played football on the opposite team and was the person I'd had to block. But we'd worn helmets, and I had never examined her features like I suddenly was Quinn's.

My finger had just reached the beauty mark high on her left cheek when a loud male voice called Quinn's name.

She jumped back as if I had the plague.

"Are you touching my sister?" the dude asked.

I hadn't seen him yet, and I knew from his higher tone that he wasn't that Chase fellow.

Quinn ran around me like a tornado rushing across the Great Plains. She held up her hands, trying to block a guy twice her size. "Liam, I ran into him. He was only making sure I was okay."

So Liam was the lone ranger—the one who hadn't followed Chase like a cub following his momma bear. I realized in that instant why Liam looked familiar. He looked like Quinn.

Liam was breathing fire over Quinn's head.

I ambled over with my arm outstretched. "I'm Maiken."

"The whole school knows who you are," Liam said kind of snidely.

"Quinn and I bumped into each other. It was my fault. I wasn't paying attention to where I was going."

Quinn planted her hands on her hips. "Liam, where are your manners?"

I held back a laugh. She sounded like she was his mother.

Liam finally shook my hand. "My brother, Carter, and I are very protective over our sister."

I grinned. "I have three sisters. So I get you."

As if that were all he needed to hear, the anger on his face washed away. "I saw you talking to Coach. We could use a tall guy like you on the team. That is if you're any good."

Quinn reared back. "You play basketball?"

I mentally scratched my head as to why she was shocked that I played ball. *Does she like that I play? Or maybe she doesn't. Then again, why do I care what she thinks?* I didn't get a chance to ponder that question before my cell phone rang.

"Sorry again. I got to run." I fished out my phone from my jacket pocket. "I'm on my way," I said to Ethan.

Emma and Ethan were waiting for me at the car.

"Maiken," Liam called. "Think about basketball."

I blew out air as I walked out in the frigid cold. Maybe playing and expending some bottled-up energy would be good for me. Otherwise, I might do something I would regret, and that something was ramming my fists into Chase.

Chapter 7

Quinn

I walked into the farm store, and Momma almost dropped the vase of flowers she was holding. "What in the world happened to you? Don't tell me you and Tessa got into a fight."

Tessa didn't fight with her fists. Her way of scratching her claws was finding ways to embarrass me like she had that morning in front of Maiken.

Liam barreled in behind me. "Chill, Mom. Seems Quinn is all feet."

"Hey, Maiken bumped into me. So it's partly his fault. Besides, you were ready to beat him up."

"No, sis," Liam said so innocently. "I was ready to send him through the glass doors when I saw his hands on you."

I rolled my eyes. My brothers talked with their fists.

Momma set down the bouquet of roses then darted into the store-room and came out with a bag of frozen carrots. "Here, put this on your eyes. It will cut down on the swelling."

I'd been examining myself in the car mirror while Liam drove us home. It seemed I was beginning to resemble a raccoon. I could only imagine what Tessa would do when she saw me or the rumors that would spread like wildfire around school. I could sulk about it, stay home until the bruises faded, or use tons of makeup. The last thing I wanted was to be called names or picked on, and Tessa wasn't the only evil person in school. The problem was I couldn't miss classes. It was hard to catch up, especially in my AP classes.

I held the frozen bag of carrots in one hand as I felt around my nose.

Momma tipped up my chin. "It's not broken, is it?"

God, I prayed not. I wiggled my nose around. "I don't think so."

Momma moved hair off my forehead. "So you mean that handsome nephew of Eleanor's?"

All I could do was smile as I thought about how hard his chest had been.

My brother Carter blew into the store. He had a way of making an entrance. Then again, he was a big boy, super muscular, more so than Liam. He also towered over Momma and me. "Are you okay, Quinn? Who did this to you?" His brown hair toppled over into his eyes.

"You called him?" I snapped at Liam, who was eating a pastry from the cake dish that was on the counter alongside the register.

I didn't need Carter to scare Maiken for no reason. Carter was exactly like my dad. He would get the shotgun out if he so much as saw a boy approaching me. Nevertheless, Maiken wouldn't even look at me if Carter started trouble.

I loved my brothers, but they could be so overprotective that I might never date. Come to think of it, I didn't know of any boy who was interested in me or would be, for that matter. Or maybe some were interested but just frightened of my brothers.

Liam shook his shaggy head. "No, I texted him." He looked at Carter. "We need to have a talk with Maiken. I think he and Chase are going to throw down, and we can't have that. With Alex gone, we need a shooting guard, a good one, and I heard Coach talking about how Maiken is a great shooting guard."

I placed the frozen bag on one eye, the cold sting making me wince. "But Alex wasn't a shooting guard." I might have been a book-worm, but I knew the game of basketball, thanks to my brothers and my dad.

"No," Liam said in between chewing. "But Chase isn't great at that position. He can move to point guard."

Knowing Tessa's brother, Chase, he wouldn't like giving up his position no matter if he did or didn't excel as a shooting guard.

"Or maybe Chase can be a small forward, and Coach can move Phil to point guard," Carter added. "Phil has the skills for point guard, and he's also the shortest of players, which suits that position."

Liam was a center for the team, so it didn't make sense for him to change positions. He had the height for a center too.

Momma resumed arranging her flowers. "Why don't you boys ask Maiken if he would like to help out with the Christmas trees? We could use a strong person like him. Maybe then you could convince him to play basketball."

I wanted to hug Momma but also scream at her. I couldn't have Maiken working on the farm. I wouldn't get my chores done. Instead, I would be watching him every second. I shivered in delight at the way he had saved me from falling, or more like saved himself from falling on top of me. My cheeks heated even with the frozen bag on my eye.

Oh my. If Father Thomas knew what I was thinking, he would add ten Our Fathers and Hail Marys to my penance.

"Don't force Maiken into playing," I said. "His father recently died. He's probably mourning right now." Momma had shared that info with me after Maiken and Eleanor had left the store.

Our family had experienced the death of our grandfather, but we'd been prepared since Grandpa had battled colon cancer, and we'd known what the end result would be.

"How?" Liam asked, still stuffing his face and drinking out of a gallon of milk.

Momma went over to Liam and snagged the carton. "Young man, where are your manners? This milk is for sale, not for you to open and drink the whole gallon."

Liam wiped his mouth with the back of his hand. "Sorry, ma'am."

No, he wasn't. He would do it again and again like always.

"His father died in combat," Momma added, refrigerating the milk in a section that was locked off to customers.

"Come on, Carter." Liam started for the door. "Let's go have a chat."

"You're not going without me." I had chores, but no way was I missing their exchange. I had to be there just in case my brothers decided to inform Maiken to stay away from me or if they got out of control with their fists. Carter had been known to punch first and ask questions later. Then again, I couldn't physically stop them, and if I were being honest, I wanted to see Maiken.

"Quinn," Momma said. "Let the boys go. I need you here."

I waltzed up to Momma, who was now behind the register. The farm store was dead for a Monday afternoon, so I didn't see the need to stay aside from the horses I had to feed. "Momma, you told me the other day that you wanted me to have fun in high school. Something about finding a boyfriend." I whispered the last part. If my brothers knew I was crushing hard on Maiken, then they wouldn't let me tag along.

Momma checked on Liam and Carter. Carter was grabbing a soda out of the fridge. "Quinn, it's not proper to chase boys. I do want you to go on your first date, but you have to let the boy ask."

"I'm not chasing him. I want to make sure Carter and Liam don't do something so that Maiken would never ask me out." I was pulling at straws. I knew Maiken wasn't interested in me by the way he'd run out of the store the other day. "I want to thank his sister Emma. She paid me a compliment, and I haven't had a chance to say thank you." I wasn't lying. Since Emma was a freshman and wasn't in any of my classes, I hadn't seen her the entire day.

Carter burped. "Quinn, you're not going. It's not a conversation for girls."

I flared my nostrils. I didn't get mad easily except when my brothers acted like cavemen.

"Young man," Momma said in her stern tone. "Quinn is going."

Carter raised one of his thick eyebrows. "You just said you wanted Quinn here."

Momma stuck her hands on her hips. "Quinn needs to see Maiken's sister."

"Yes, ma'am," Carter said as he headed outside.

I kissed her on the cheek then hurried out and hopped into Carter's old, beat-up Chevy truck.

We lived six miles down the road from the Maxwell estate. So within ten minutes, we were wheeling into their driveway. On a beautiful summer day, we could have walked a wooded path from our farm to the Maxwell home and shaved a mile off the distance. At least we'd had that option until Eleanor and Martin had purchased all the land within a five-mile radius of their estate the previous year. Now the path was closed off, mainly because of the homes that were being built for their sons.

My belly pricked with nerves as Carter banked around the fountain to stop across from the front porch.

"They must've had this paved recently," Liam said. "Wait, is any of the family in a wheelchair?"

A ramp jutted out from the porch, which was new. The last time I'd been there was last winter when I'd used the lake to ice-skate.

Carter killed the engine. "Yeah, Kody's girl. Her brother is in a wheelchair. You know the dude who owns the motorcycle shop."

"Lowell Ryan?" Liam asked. Liam wasn't one to pay attention to the local gossip at church. We'd heard of the family when their mother died of breast cancer years ago.

The front door opened, and my stomach started doing flips, not because I was about to see Maiken, but because teaming up on Maiken wasn't such a good idea. My brothers could be quite overbearing.

The eldest son, Kade Maxwell, came out. I quietly sighed. The four Maxwell brothers were handsome, but I thought Kade was the yummy one. I liked how tall he was, like Maiken. I liked his honey-colored hair, which was also thick like Maiken's, although Maiken had more blond than Kade.

Carter got out of the truck. Liam exited too. I didn't move. I'd been sitting in between my brothers with my feet glued to the floorboard. Carter had one of those old trucks that had one long front seat with no console.

I casually checked myself in the rearview mirror. *Oh my God.* Why had I even pushed to come? The area around my eyes had darkened. The next day would be even worse.

But I was already there, so I couldn't exactly look like an oddball and stay in the truck.

"Hey, man," Kade said to Carter.

They gave each other a manly hug.

"We're looking for your cousin," Liam piped in.

Kade folded his arms over his Henley. "Which one?" His tone was reserved, sounding as though he were ready to get mad at someone.

I waved as I sidled up to Liam and Carter. "We need to talk to Maiken."

Kade took on a shocked expression when he set his eyes on me. "Please tell me he didn't give you those black eyes."

I smiled as if I were proud that I had been branded like a raccoon. "Accident."

Carter stood on the bottom step. "We would like to offer him a job helping out with the Christmas tree sales."

"Let's go inside," Kade said. "I'll get Maiken."

I'd only been in the Maxwell house maybe twice, and both times, I'd walked in with my mouth hanging open. That day wasn't any different. A crystal chandelier hung from the ceiling in the foyer, and another one dangled in the enormous dining room off to my left.

Kade disappeared down a hall somewhere.

I peeked into the quaint sitting room on my right. A fire crackled.

Liam tapped me on the shoulder. "Don't be nosy."

"Says the brother with no manners," I teased.

Carter shoved his hands into the pocket of his winter coat. "Stop it."

Footsteps clamored on the honey wood floor before Kade reappeared. "Maiken will be right out." He waved his hand toward the kitchen. "Make yourself at home."

Directly ahead of us was the spacious gourmet kitchen. Momma had gushed about how she wanted a kitchen like her friend's. Dad would always respond to Momma with, "You have the best farm kitchen in the state."

Whether we did or not, it didn't have stainless-steel appliances or a stove with eight burners and two large ovens. I'd only been in Tessa Stevens's house two times that I could remember when I was in grade school, and her kitchen was just as large. I guess the rich folk had a standard for kitchens, although I didn't place the Maxwells in my definition of rich folk—snooty and mean. Mr. and Mrs. Maxwell were the kindest human beings I knew outside of my family.

Carter, Liam, and I settled around the island, when Maiken sauntered in. His jaw fell to the floor when we locked eyes. Then he regarded Liam and Carter, his attention lingering on Carter as though he knew Carter could be trouble.

"I'll be down in the media room with the others," Kade said to Maiken.

"Is Emma here?" I asked Kade.

"She's not," Maiken chimed in.

"She's with her mom and my wife," Kade added. "They won't be back for a while." Then he was gone.

Maiken raised his big hands, keeping his gaze on Carter. "Your sister and I bumped into each other."

All three boys were around the same height. The differences were in their arms and chests. Liam and Maiken had muscles, but they were leaner than Carter.

Sliding his hands into his jeans pockets, Maiken glanced at me. "I'm sorry. Are you okay?"

"Did you know that the mask of a raccoon helps other raccoons to identify with one another?" Inwardly, I screamed at myself to shut up.

Liam busted out laughing. Maiken's jaw slackened.

Carter draped his arm over my shoulders. "That's our sister. She's a wealth of information."

My face became as hot as the campfires we sat around in the summertime. *Stupid. Stupid. Stupid.*

Liam's laugh faded. "So, we're here to offer you a job. We also want you to consider playing basketball."

As if the word had some type of calming effect on Maiken, he slumped his shoulders. Then he grinned wide, and oh, my belly did five tumbles. Zac Efron had nothing on this boy.

Carter let me go. "We're the premier farm for Christmas trees, and we need your guns."

I could see the outline of Maiken's guns, or rather muscles, through his long-sleeve T-shirt, which had the word Army ironed on across his chest. *Celia would be so jealous right now.* I was standing across from the most handsome boy I'd ever seen.

"How much does it pay?" Maiken asked.

"Minimum wage," Carter said. "Weekends are the busiest. Can you start this weekend?" Carter was being his usual pushy self. Dad had taught him to always be presumptuous when trying to sell. When he did, it was hard for a person to say no.

Maiken set his scrumptious blue eyes on me, and my heart went haywire. I prayed no one could see it beating out of my chest. I did have my winter coat unzipped, so it was possible to see movement through my sweater.

Carter waved a hand in the air. "Dude, if you're so much as drooling over Quinn, I will cut off your legs."

I kicked my brother in the shin. Maiken couldn't see that since the island was separating us. And he wasn't admiring my breasts, which was what Carter was getting at. At least I didn't think Maiken was, although he had the first time I'd met him at the farm store.

Still, I didn't want Carter to start a brawl in the beautiful and expensive kitchen. Momma would have a fit, and Daddy would be livid if he had to pay for the damage.

Casually, Maiken looked away. "I'll consider the offer." Then he turned to Liam. "Coach gave me until tomorrow to make my decision on playing. But why are you so desperate to have me play? You don't know me or what I'm capable of."

Liam shrugged. "I heard you're good."

Disgust washed over Maiken's face. "Gossip at Kensington should make the *Guinness Book of World Records.*"

I wouldn't disagree with that statement. I wanted to say something, but I was afraid I might drop a stupid comment like the raccoon one. Nervousness was a funny thing. Most people clammed up when they were nervous, but not me. I rattled off facts about nothing.

Carter scratched his head, a sign he was getting bored. "Tell you what? Since you have until tomorrow to decide on basketball, we'll give you until then to decide on our job offer."

I kicked Carter again.

He eyed me with a crease in between his brows. "We need help, and we can't wait any longer. We have a small window to sell trees."

Carter took after Daddy, always worrying about the farm and money and how we were going to pay the bills if the farm didn't produce or if something happened to our farm animals. We'd lost several chickens last winter to cold.

"That's fair," Maiken said. "I'll let you know then."

Carter started for the door. Liam and I didn't.

"Please, man," Liam said. "Seriously consider basketball. We had a great chance to go to the state finals in Springfield when Alex was alive. Maybe with you on the team, we still could."

"Liam. Quinn. Let's go," Carter said from the foyer.

Since Emma wasn't there, I had no other excuse to stay. I wanted to talk to Maiken, but I knew my nerves would get in the way. Sure, I could talk to other boys, mostly the ones in my advanced placement classes and the ones who were as shy as me when it came to talking to the opposite sex.

Liam and I obeyed Carter and headed for the door.

"Quinn," Maiken called. "Can I talk to you for a minute?"

Carter strapped on his big-brother face. Liam didn't, which

surprised me. What was even more shocking was that Liam leaned in and whispered, "Convince him to play. I'll take care of Carter. We'll be in the truck."

For the first time ever, Liam wasn't ready to beat up a boy who wanted to talk to me.

Reluctantly, Carter left with Liam, leaving Maiken and me in complete silence.

The voice in my head was warning me not to say something stupid, but I couldn't promise I wouldn't. Holding my breath, I wrung my hands together so he wouldn't see how nervous I was.

Casually, he leaned against the arched doorway. His look sucked me into the deep depths of his blue orbs. "I'm sorry for your eyes."

"Not your fault." I gave myself a mental high five for not stuttering.

"So you like basketball?" he asked.

I swallowed hard. A boy had never asked me about sports. "Did you know that the Celtics have won the most NBA Championships?" *Shut up, brain.*

He gave me the most heart-stopping smile. "So you do like the sport."

"Y-you really sh-should play," I stuttered out.

He inched toward me. "Why is that, Quinn?"

If he came any closer, I might throw myself at him.

He settled two short inches from me. *Wow!* I didn't recall him smelling as if he'd bathed in aftershave. I couldn't pinpoint the scent, though. Regardless, he was making me dizzy.

I pointed at the door. "I sh-should go. My brothers." I had to stop stuttering.

"You didn't answer my question." That time when he spoke, I detected a hint of a Southern drawl, which I hadn't before, not that I'd heard him speak much.

I swept my gaze from his abs to his jaw then his lips. I lingered there for a moment before meeting his eyes. My pulse went *boom* and *bang* several times because of the bad thoughts I was having over a boy. "Bad thoughts" was a relative term depending on one's definition. Celia might not have considered rubbing her hands over Maiken's chest bad, but in my world, it was salacious, or so I'd been taught.

Momma had always said that it wasn't proper to have sexual thoughts of another unless I loved him. I didn't love Maiken. I didn't even know him. *So why am I thinking of him naked?*

Carter blew his horn.

If I stayed, I might do something like kiss Maiken. That wouldn't be proper, and it would be extremely embarrassing. I wasn't what my granny called some girls—a hussy.

I turned and practically sprinted for the door. Maiken called my name, but I didn't stop. I was definitely going to plead with Momma and Daddy to let me stay home from school indefinitely. After all, I had black eyes, my cheeks seemed to stay permanently red around Maiken, and my body felt as if it were on fire. I would've liked to say I was coming down with the flu, but I knew deep down that wasn't remotely true.

Chapter 8

Maiken

The moment I walked into school the next morning, I felt dizzy. I couldn't pinpoint the reason why. I'd attended several schools since my dad had been in the military, and I'd never felt as though I didn't belong. Actually, I'd never cared or paid attention to the whispers and gossip around me. Yet at Kensington, I couldn't shake the bad feeling I had that something was about to happen.

Ethan and Emma were with me as we skirted around students in the halls on our way to our lockers. It was unusual for freshmen to have lockers in the same hall as sophomores at Kensington. Apparently, the freshmen had lockers in another wing of the school. But when we'd enrolled, all the freshmen lockers were taken.

Emma loved the idea of being close to me. So did Ethan for that matter. We tried to stick together as much as we could.

Emma toyed with her braided hair. "So you apologized to Quinn for giving her black eyes, right?"

The three of us settled at our lockers.

Before I could respond, Tessa Stevens invaded my personal space. I wasn't a fan of people getting so close unless it was on the basketball court.

Emma bared her teeth.

I could feel my forehead wrinkling at my sister. I knew she was protective, but I'd never seen her so offended by a girl talking to me. After all, Emma had even said I needed to date sometime.

Tessa licked her bright-red lips, ignoring Emma. "So, Maiken, I'm having a holiday party the weekend before Christmas and would like for you to come."

Ethan messed with his unruly brown hair. I swore my brother didn't know what a comb or a brush was. His idea of hygiene was to shower and let the air handle the rest. "If Maiken goes, my sister and I go too."

Outrage plagued the pretty girl, and she was pretty—silky black hair, eyes to match, curves, and small breasts. Yet her pushy attitude masked her beauty.

I opened my locker. "Thanks for the offer, but no thanks. I have to work."

My siblings angled their heads. I hadn't told them about working at the Thompson farm. Emma had been out with Lacey and my mom when Quinn and her brothers had stopped by. And Ethan had taken Marcus and Jasper for a hike through the woods. Kade had gotten stuck babysitting the rest of my clan. Well, he'd actually offered. I hadn't argued since I'd had homework to do. I had missed a lot of school since Dad died, and I was trying to catch up.

Tessa handed me an invitation. "Take it in case you change your mind."

I didn't have a chance to touch the small white envelope before Emma snagged it from Tessa.

"Does that mean we're invited?" Emma asked with excitement dripping off her. My sister was all about parties. She always loved to plan our birthday parties.

Tessa jutted out her chin. "Why not? It's a giving and cheery time of year." Then she glided down the hall and was sucked up by her friends.

I poked my head in my locker and took a breath.

Emma grabbed my arm. "I might sound hypocritical, but let's go to the party. I don't want you to go near her, but I want to have some fun."

"I'll go out with her," Ethan added.

"What about Hannah?" He had been whining about missing his girlfriend in North Carolina.

Ethan's features tightened. "Hannah broke up with me. She said something about how long-distance relationships don't work. Don't say you're sorry either." His tone was hard.

I wanted to hug him, but it was clear he wasn't ready to talk about Hannah. Besides, we needed to blow off some steam.

I closed my locker. "I'm not going anywhere near Tessa."

Emma scanned the hall. "Then take Quinn to the party. That will show Tessa you're not interested in her."

I hadn't had a chance to see who was around or who was listening to our conversation. Frankly, I could care less about gossip anyway. But after Emma's statement, I surveyed the students nearby and found Quinn standing several lockers down and across from me.

She blinked my way, and pain gripped my chest. I felt awful that I'd given her two black eyes. Nevertheless, I didn't know what to make of the girl who had pin-straight butterscotch hair. She'd rendered me speechless the day before when she'd spouted off facts about the Celtics. I'd wondered all night what else she knew about the game. Maybe her knowledge of the game was the reason she'd been surprised that I played ball.

Tessa waltzed up to Quinn, and everyone in the hall stopped what they were doing. "What happened to you? Did one of your pigs get the best of you?" She laughed hysterically.

Celia, who was hanging with Quinn, said, "Get lost, Tessa."

"You're just as frumpy as she is. Oh, and you're off the cheer-leading team," Tess said with pride.

Celia rolled her eyes. "I already quit. Remember?"

Quinn hugged the books in her arms as though she were trying hard not to give Tessa a shiner.

Tessa pursed her lips. "Both of you are lowlifes." She tossed her hair over her shoulder and left Celia and Quinn standing in the dust.

I clenched my fists to prevent myself from saying something. I didn't get in the middle of fights, especially where girls were concerned. But girls became a memory when I spotted Chase bobbing his way toward me.

The warning bell rang.

Emma and Ethan said goodbye, oblivious to Chase storming through the crowd, which was dispersing in all directions like rats in a sewer.

I was only two doors down from my first-period class, so I didn't have far to go.

With his wet mud-colored hair, he settled in front of me, crossing his arms over his letter jacket. "We don't need you on the team. So stay away."

When I'd gotten out of bed that morning, I'd made the decision not to play. I'd decided to take the year off and work. I'd also decided that I would take the job offer at the farm for the holidays, but only because I liked Liam. I wasn't sure yet about his brother, Carter. Not only that, I'd overheard Mom talking with her sister about moving to Georgia, but not until the school year was over, which was one reason I didn't want to get too involved in sports only to be uprooted once again.

But considering Chase's glower, I was wavering in my decision. Maybe I would show Coach Dean what skills I had on the court. Playing would also keep my shooting game in tip-top shape.

I was about to reply when I spied Quinn and Celia walking over.

Chase followed my line of sight. Then he let out a laugh that could probably be heard in the next town over.

Quinn's cheeks turned red.

Celia snarled. "Say one smart-ass thing, Chase, and I'll knee you in the balls."

Chase didn't pay Celia any attention. Instead, his laughter died as he rested a finger underneath Quinn's chin. "Who did this to you?" He sounded as if he cared. "Tell me, and I'll take care of them."

Quinn's forehead furrowed.

Mine did as well.

In one breath, Chase was an ass, and then in the next, he was genuinely concerned. Whatever his reasons were, I didn't like him touching her.

I grabbed Chase's arm. "Leave her alone."

Chase shrugged out of my hold. "Or what, Maxwell? If you think you can swagger into Kensington and take over, you're wrong. I own this school. So don't get any ideas that you or your siblings can do what you want here."

I laughed. I wasn't one to get into fights or even throw the first punch. I tried to mind my own business, play basketball, take care of my siblings, help Mom, and hang out with my friends. But I didn't have any friends at that school. I wasn't playing basketball, and for some reason, I didn't want to mind my own business. Since my dad had passed, anger had been building inside me, bubbling and simmering underneath the grief and sadness.

Whether or not Chase was an excuse to unleash my ire, he deserved to be taken down a notch.

Before I could respond, Quinn's small, soft hand was in mine. "He's not worth it."

Chase's face twisted as he laughed. The sound felt like a sharp knife piercing my skin. "Quinn, you know very well you don't stand a chance against my sister, Tessa. She will swallow Maxwell up and spit him out, and then he'll be mincemeat to you. Besides, you're better with me."

Quinn giggled as her hand tightened around mine.

I almost choked. Things were starting to make sense. Chase was just as domineering and cocky as his sister. Still, he sounded confident that I would date his sister. Hell would freeze over before that happened.

Quinn made a low noise in the back of her throat.

I should've defended her honor, but she had me riveted to the floor. I liked how her hand felt in mine—soft, calm, and delicate. For someone who came off as shy and stuttering and spat out facts easily, she was certainly showing a side of her that I would guess was shocking her more than me.

She squeezed my hand as tightly as she could. "Your sister can do all the damage she wants." No mincing words that time.

"Hell, yeah," Celia shouted.

The hall had thinned out, but a few onlookers hung back, watching.

Chase's nostrils were moving in and out. "For your sake, Quinn, I hope she doesn't do too much to you. We all know how you run anytime she picks on you."

Her grip tightened even more on my hand.

I got in Chase's face. "How pathetic that you have to stoop to threatening a girl. If you want to take this outside, I would be more than happy to oblige."

Quinn let go of my hand, slipped in between Chase and me, and used her whole body to push me back. I went willingly, or else I would have shoved the dude into a locker. I didn't have anything to lose except disappointing my mom, which I didn't want to do. But she would understand if I were defending a girl's honor. Hell, my dad would've been proud of me.

"T-tell your s-sister she can give me her best shot."

I smiled as Quinn exhibited her toughness through her nerves. I was also shouting "way to go" in my head.

Chase studied Quinn as if she were nonhuman.

A teacher, short and chubby, cleared her throat. "Quinn, inside. The final bell is about to ring."

Without so much as a passing glance, Quinn scurried into class.

Chase and I were in a standoff until the bell rang.

"This isn't over," Chase announced in a hushed whisper.

I didn't think it was. "I'll see you on the court, then."

He reared back, shook his head, then stalked off.

I couldn't say what he was thinking, but one thing was certain—he would see me on the basketball court.

Chapter 9

Quinn

The entire school day dragged by like the slow-moving turtle I had in my aquarium at home. I felt as if I hadn't been able to breathe since I walked through the school doors that morning, actually since Tessa had practically thrown herself at Maiken in the hall. It wasn't hard to hear that she'd invited him to her annual holiday gala. Her parents always hosted the rich, richer, and richest to their estate during the holidays. My family wasn't on that list. I couldn't say I was surprised that Tessa had asked Maiken. After all, he was a Maxwell, and they had money, or at least Eleanor and Martin were wealthy.

Regardless of stature, I'd been searching out Maiken any chance I had. I wanted to apologize to him. I'd never intended to grab his hand. Frankly, that move had shocked the lights out of me. I wasn't that type of girl. But for some odd reason, when Chase had been throwing down the gauntlet at Maiken then me, my hand had had a mind of its own.

Normally, my modus operandi was to cower. But I realized my breaking point was Maiken. He somehow had given me the courage to stand up to Chase. I wasn't sure if it was a fluke or not.

Regardless, I tapped my chest a couple of times, took in a gulp of the stale air that always lingered in the sports complex, then expelled it from my lungs.

I could hear the cheerleaders practicing inside the gym. They weren't as loud as the whistle Coach Dean kept blowing. I peeked in through the sliver of a glass pane on the door. I was there to meet Liam and nothing more. He was my ride home.

Tessa and the rest of the cheerleaders were watching head cheerleader Brianna Masters do a routine.

My gaze shifted from the squad to the court. My heart did a little dance when I spotted Maiken going in for a layup only to be blocked by Chase. I was curious if Maiken had decided to play because I'd told him to. As soon as that thought entered my mind, it left quickly. The only one who actually did as I said was my dog, Bo.

The boys pushed each other before Chase waved at Maiken in a taunting gesture.

Coach Dean blew his whistle. For a second, neither boy moved. They just continued staring each other down. I wouldn't even begin to guess who would win a fight. Chase and Maiken were the same build.

The high-pitched sound of the whistle trilled again. Liam darted down the court to Maiken and Chase. I rushed into the gym as if I could stop a brawl. The cheerleaders seemed to be holding their breath as Coach Dean stomped to midcourt.

"Stevens and Maxwell," Coach yelled. "Get your asses over here."

"Maiken, this isn't the way to get on the team," Liam said.

I spotted Celia in the stands, sitting by herself as she too waited for one of the boys to throw the first punch. I climbed up two rows and joined her, biting my lip.

She quickly regarded me. "Maiken would win for sure."

Maybe so, but I didn't want to see anyone get hurt.

Maiken wiped the sweat from his forehead with his T-shirt. The anger on his face could probably frighten one of my farm animals.

Maiken jogged to center court. Chase took his time. He too had tons of tension jumping off him.

I wanted to scream at them both. But I wasn't the right person to knock some sense into them. I was the one who ran from confrontation, although I hadn't that morning with Chase. As I recalled how I'd stood up to him, I felt as if a pack of wolves were chomping on the inside of my stomach, mainly because if Chase had relayed my message to Tessa, I wasn't ready for her to give me her best shot. I wished I could take back what I'd said.

The team huddled around Coach Dean. He launched into plays rather than reprimand anyone, although he had no tolerance for fighting. He'd almost kicked Liam off the baseball team one year for doing just that with a boy who no longer attended Kensington.

"I can't believe I ever wanted to be a cheerleader," Celia said in a low voice. "Look how some of them appear scared."

"Well, Tessa has that effect," I said. Brianna wasn't much different, but she wasn't as bad as Tessa, although Brianna didn't take flack from Tessa, and the only reason Tessa didn't spit fire at Brianna was due to Brianna's seniority as captain of the squad.

Celia leaned back to rest her elbows on the bleachers behind her. "Was I like that when I was cheerleading?"

"I don't know. I didn't pay much attention." Only because I was so mad at her for ruining our friendship. "What are you doing in the gym anyway? I thought you were going to help your mom at the bakery."

Her mom owned a bakery in town that was always busy from early morning to early afternoon. She closed at about the time school let out then baked and prepped for the crowd the next day. My mom often purchased baked goods from her to sell in the farm store.

"I wanted to talk to Liam and apologize for coming on too strong," she said.

I sought out my brother, who was facing me and standing next to Maiken. But Liam became a dot in my vision when Maiken looked over and waved at me.

"He likes you," Celia said. "And by the way, I know I've said this a million times today, but I'm proud of how you stood up to Chase. Oh, and how you held Maiken's hand." She let out a dreamy sigh.

I couldn't believe myself either. His hand was strong, big, and warm. I'd wanted to hold his hand forever.

Celia tapped me on the arm. "Here comes trouble."

I flinched out of my daydreaming to find Tessa ambling our way.

Argh!

She fixed her high ponytail. "You'll never get him, Quinn. Remember, Quinn never wins."

"He d-d-doesn't like you." I used my church voice.

She pouted, sticking out her red bottom lip. She always wore bright-red lipstick. "Aw, she still stutters." Then her face turned mean and evil. "Come anywhere near my territory, and the next three years of high school will be hell for you." She left before I could respond.

Then again, I didn't think I could speak. She had that effect on me. *What happened to sticking up for yourself?* I couldn't worry about that. What bothered me more was what Tessa would do if I continued to show interest in Maiken. So far, words had been her only weapon, and she belittled me every chance she got. But I was afraid she would do more to win Maiken over. Sure, Emma had said her brother was only being polite to Tessa when he'd smiled at her, but he was a boy, and Tessa was a pretty girl.

Maybe Momma was right. I should skate again. Maybe then I could beat Tessa at something and shut her up so she would leave me alone. But as the thought occurred to me, I dismissed it for all the reasons I'd listed—money, time, and my schoolwork would suffer.

"She isn't going to let up. Is she?" I asked Celia.

"Unfortunately, Tessa will always be a thorn in your side unless you show her you can stand up to her."

I believed I was damned if I did and damned if I didn't. If I stood up to her, she would only get witchier. If I ignored her like I had been, she would continue to lash out here and there. The key was not to bring attention to myself by talking to Maiken or showing that I was interested in him.

You're supposed to have fun in high school. What kind of fun is that? You already held his hand. He waved at you. He seems different than the other boys who just want to get in a girl's pants.

Or maybe Maiken had stuck up for me with Chase because he felt sorry that he'd given me black eyes. Maybe that was why he'd waved at me a few minutes ago.

My dilemma vanished when Maiken came over with Liam in tow.

"Maiken is going to work at the farm." Liam sounded excited, as if he'd just gotten the new truck he'd been wanting.

Celia and I swapped a wide-eyed look. Then Celia hopped up. "It's time to get Maiken familiar with farm animals."

Maiken's fear shined brighter than the sheen of sweat coating his face. "Is there an initiation before I can start? Aren't I only helping customers load trees in their cars?"

Liam, Celia, and I busted out laughing.

Liam slapped Maiken on the back. "Part of helping is cleaning out the pigsty."

Maiken's jaw came unhinged. "You're kidding, right?"

It was fun to tease Maiken, but I didn't want to scare him off. "Of course he's kidding."

Chase hustled over.

Maiken blocked him from my view. "What do you want?" His tone was brittle.

Chase scooted around Maiken. "Quinn, I wanted to apologize for this morning."

If I was surprised that Maiken would be working at the farm, I was even more dumbfounded that Chase was apologizing. Then I realized Liam or Carter must've heard what happened earlier that day and had probably put the fear of God into Chase.

When Chase regarded Liam, I knew I was right. But I wasn't about to condemn Chase for his apology, even though it was forced. So I said thank you like a proper girl would and smiled.

He left without even spitting out barbs at Maiken like he had before school. I should have also thanked Chase for being his evil self. He'd forced me to step out of my comfort zone. But I tabled that thought and focused on Maiken, who was shrugging on his sweatshirt and collecting his sports bag.

Celia nudged me with her shoulder. "Go talk to him."

I could count on one hand the number of boys I'd liked and not had the nerve to talk to—one, Alex Baker. I did want to apologize to

Maiken, though, but when Liam and Celia strolled out of the gym, leaving Maiken and me alone, my mouth became bone dry.

The other players and cheerleaders had left. Even Coach Dean had packed up and was nowhere to be seen.

Maiken hiked his bag over his shoulder as he closed the distance between us. His hair was damp with sweat, his cheeks were rose-colored, and his wolfish grin was heart-stopping. "So do I need to know about the farm animals or clean the pigsty?"

I smothered a giggle as my nerves took over. "Did you know pigs are smarter than dogs?"

He let out a loud laugh, warm and infectious. "My sister Charlotte would love you."

"How many siblings do you have?" Momma had mentioned a number, but all I could remember when she started talking about how the Maxwell family was growing was something about fielding a team.

"Seven," he said as we walked out of the gym.

Silence followed us outside and into the freezing cold. Maiken visibly shivered.

I couldn't say I was immune to the cold temps, but they didn't bother me as much as they would someone who had moved there from a warmer climate.

Without thinking, I grasped his hand then froze like an ice sculpture. I swallowed the fur ball that had suddenly collected in my throat. *Twice in one day.* The first time I'd held his hand might have been an accident, but the second time might mean it was becoming a habit—one that would keep a smile on my face and tingles in my belly.

Regardless, I immediately withdrew my hand. "I d-didn't mean to do that."

He grinned, and his blue eyes brightened like the sun at dawn. "Don't take this the wrong way, but you're different."

I pursed my lips, hunching into myself. It was hard for a shy girl like me not to take that the wrong way. Not only that, but one of the football players had said the very same thing to me before he asked me out when those nasty rumors were going around school about me being an easy target to get under the covers.

"Did I offend you?" Maiken asked.

Normally, I would've melted like warm butter on a biscuit when I heard his voice, but I spotted Liam pointing a finger in Celia's face.

Maiken followed my line of sight.

"Excuse me." I rushed over to Liam and Celia, clenching my teeth. I hardly got angry, but my brother could be a donkey's butt, and he knew better than to treat a girl like he was treating Celia, who was snarling at him. At least she wasn't shrinking under him, something I would've done if a boy acted high and mighty and belligerent with me.

That's not true. You stood up to Chase. One time only.

Maiken followed on my heels.

"What's going on?" I directed the question at Liam.

Celia dashed a tear away with her fingers. "It's nothing. I have to go." She jogged back to the building.

Liam stormed into his truck and started the engine.

I was about to hop in when Maiken's voice stopped me. "Quinn, did I say something wrong?"

I shouldn't have been agitated that he'd said I was different. But different to me meant weird, shy, and slow. I might've been shy, but I wasn't slow or weird.

"No," I lied. I didn't see the point in explaining myself because he would probably laugh at my reasoning. Besides, the nerve he'd hit was a little sore.

"Quinn," Liam said. "Let's go. Maiken, be at the farm store at seven tonight. You can meet my dad and fill out the paperwork."

I waved at Maiken as I got into the truck. I had every intention of grilling Liam on why he and Celia were arguing, but I knew he wouldn't tell me. So I strapped myself in and sent a text to Celia to call me later.

Boys. Argh! I was beginning to think branching out and having fun, as Momma had put it, was more of a headache than anything, particularly if my heart was on the line.

Chapter 10

Maiken

The farm store was empty save for Mr. Thompson and me. He stood behind the counter, perusing my employment application as though he'd found something interesting.

This was my first job, so I didn't have any references or other employment. "Did I miss a box or a line?"

He lifted his brown gaze, wearing a mean expression, much like the one I'd seen on Carter the other day when he'd assumed I was ogling his sister. I hadn't exactly been drooling over Quinn. If I were being honest, I was kind of scared of how Quinn was making me feel. The boy-girl thing was new for me.

I remembered when my brother Ethan had first started chasing girls at the age of thirteen. He would always brag about this girl or that girl and how pretty she was or how one girl in particular, Hannah, had made his stomach queasy in a good way. Maybe I was a late bloomer. Maybe Quinn was my Hannah.

"So, you're a Maxwell." Mr. Thompson sounded apprehensive as if I were a demon about to wreak havoc on his farm.

It was my turn to knit my brows together. "Is that a problem?"

He shrugged. "It won't be if you work hard and don't bring trouble with you."

I wasn't sure why he assumed I would bring trouble. "With all due respect, sir, I don't see how loading Christmas trees for customers would be a problem."

He studied me, creases fanning out from the corners of his eyes. "There's bad history in this town with the Maxwell boys."

I'd heard of some of my cousins' high school brawls, in particular the one that had landed Kody in a coma. But I wasn't planning on following in their footsteps.

"Sir, I promise I will be the model employee." My tone was respectful, even though I didn't like that he was comparing me to my cousins.

The doorbell dinged.

Mr. Thompson slipped my application into a drawer beneath the counter. "The job starts tomorrow."

Liam waltzed in, wearing a thick flannel shirt over muddy jeans. His boots were equally as dirty, and work gloves covered his big hands.

"What time exactly?" I asked Mr. Thompson.

"We have basketball practice, Pop," Liam said. "So five."

Mr. Thompson grabbed his ball cap. "That works. Son, show Maiken around to get the lay of the land." Then his stocky form faded as he went into a back room.

Liam swatted my arm. "Come on. We'll start with the Christmas trees."

I shoved my hands into my coat pockets as we headed out, the bell ringing as we did. "Your dad doesn't like my cousins. Does he?"

He chuckled. "Let's just say that my dad prefers to see fights in a ring and not on his farm. We had a high school kid work on the farm a few years back, and he had enemies. The end result was a broken fence and cops. It's bad for business."

I had no plans to fight anyone.

"Dude, just do your job, and he'll leave you alone. Heck, if you're the perfect employee, he might even offer you a permanent job as a farmhand."

Uh, no. I wanted to make money, but shoveling shit out of a pigsty or corralling a herd of cows wasn't my ideal job. I wasn't afraid of hard work, nor was I some rich kid who thought I couldn't get my hands dirty. I'd changed enough diapers and helped Mom and Dad with other chores around the house and yard. But farm animals, in particular horses, didn't excite me. One had almost bitten off my finger when I was a kid.

Liam waved a hand in front of my face. "Dude, you look as white as the snow on the ground. Are you afraid of animals?"

"I like dogs," I said. We'd had a dog when I was a tike, but with eight kids in the family, animals were too much trouble according to Mom.

Liam busted out laughing. "Our animals won't hurt you. They're more afraid of you anyway."

We walked along a short wooden fence. A gravel lot was on one side, and rolling snow-covered hills were on the other. Eventually, we came to a stop outside a lit pergola that was home to a myriad of different sizes of Christmas trees. The strong scent of pine hung in the air.

A German shepherd trotted up to Liam. "Hey, Bo."

I held out my hand for Bo to sniff me. Instead, the dog licked my hand.

"See, man," Liam said. "No worries."

I wanted to say that Bo was a dog, not a horse, but a car turned into the parking lot. Tires crunched over the snow as the headlights blinded me.

"Bo, go see Quinn." Liam held out his hand toward a hut about ten yards down. The dog obeyed, wagging his tail as he took off.

I wasn't wagging a tail, but my body perked up at the mention of Quinn's name. I peeked around the pergola to get a glimpse of her, but I didn't see anyone in the hut. I made a mental note to apologize to her before I left or at least find out why she'd gotten so quiet when we'd walked out of the gym. I knew she had been preoccupied with Liam and Celia, who had been arguing. But that was after she'd gotten quiet when I said she was different. My assessment of her didn't mean she was weird. Different was good in my world. *She doesn't know that.*

The SUV came to a stop next to Liam and me. Then Chase Stevens hopped out of the driver's side.

Every muscle in me tensed as Mr. Thompson's words flitted through my brain.

"Maiken, why don't you go see Quinn," Liam said. "I'll handle this customer."

I had to give Liam props for reading my body language, although he already knew Chase and I were destined to brawl. We'd almost fought on the court earlier that day. Still, I didn't want to start off at a new school fighting with someone, but I wasn't about to take Chase's shit either.

I stood rooted to my spot close to a tree. Hell if I was leaving. Granted, Liam and I had just spoken about how his dad didn't like fights on the farm. But I wasn't a dog Liam could bark orders to.

Chase pulled down his knitted cap as he pursed his lips. "Liam, what the fuck is he doing here? Are you two best buds now?"

I got the impression Chase and Liam were or had been tight at one point in their lives.

"What do you want, Chase?" Liam asked. "Your mom already bought your tree."

Chase scanned the lot. "I'm here to talk to Quinn."

I snorted. He'd already apologized to Quinn in the gym earlier that day. So what could he possibly want to talk to her about?

Liam widened his stance. "What's the sudden interest in my sister?"

If Chase so much as spat out that he wanted to ask her on a date, I would punch him. He wasn't touching her.

"That's none of your business, Thompson," Chase said in a some-what reserved tone.

Liam took one step then two until he was nose to nose with Chase. "My sister is my business. If you don't want Carter and me sticking a crowbar up your ass, then I suggest you tell me now."

Bo barked, causing all three of us to look at the German shepherd that was walking up with Quinn.

Quinn clapped her hands. "Hush, Bo."

Bo sat on his haunches as Quinn asked, "What's going on?" The wind lifted strands of her hair off her shoulders.

Liam moved back from Chase. "Nothing. Chase was just leaving."

Quinn raised an eyebrow. "Why don't I believe you?"

The four of us were in somewhat of a circle with Bo's nose poking through in between Quinn and Chase. Actually, Chase was too close to her in my book.

I drilled my gaze into Chase. "We were talking about basketball. Weren't we, Chase?" I wasn't a liar and hardly stretched the truth, yet there I was lying to a girl I'd only recently met.

"We were," Chase confirmed as he removed an envelope from the inside of his coat pocket. "Quinn, first, I want again apologize for the way I treated you in school this morning."

The lights on a tree blinked behind Quinn, or maybe blaring colored lights were flashing in my head.

Chase cleared his throat. "That wasn't proper on my part. I would also like to invite you to my family's holiday gala." He handed the envelope to Quinn. "I would like for you to come as my guest." His tone was disgustingly sweet.

I felt the need to wash the slime off me.

With a shaky hand, she took the envelope. "Th-thank you."

"She's not going to a party with you." Venom dripped from Liam's voice.

Quinn jerked her head at Liam. "You don't speak for me."

Chase plastered on a cheeky grin.

My eyes widened at how confident she was when speaking to her brother. I liked her shyness. That was one feature that made Quinn so unique and appealing to me, but seeing her stand up to her brother told me she wouldn't let someone like Chase walk all over her, and that made me relax a tiny bit.

Then her eyes found mine as though she wanted my input.

I couldn't speak for her or tell her what to do, even though I wanted to say, "don't go with him. I'll be your date." But I'd never asked a girl out before, and I wasn't about to start now just because I was jealous of Chase, which was surprising me. I'd never been jealous before. Yet in that awkward moment, I wanted to tell Chase to take a hike because if he so much as held her hand, I would seriously poke out his eyes.

Liam's face contorted as he glowered at Chase. "What's your angle? You've never been interested in my sister. You're up to something."

"What would I be up to?" Chase asked. "It's my parents' party. And why can't a guy ask a girl out? So what if she's your sister. She's pretty." He lowered his gaze to Quinn. "You are." He sounded genuine. "I've always had a thing for you since we were little."

I mentally rolled my eyes. He was playing the *I've known her longer* card.

Quinn toyed with the envelope. "Why haven't you asked me out before now?"

I closed my hands into fists, and Liam hunched his shoulders. Bo nudged his nose into Quinn's hand.

"Honestly, because of your brothers. Why don't you think no guy has approached you other than the airheads who thought the rumor of you being easy were true?"

"A-all thanks to y-your sister." She pursed her lips. "I don't know if I believe you."

Oh man, maybe I was a weirdo, but Quinn's stuttering was doing things to my body in a good way.

Chase grabbed a strand of her hair that was blowing in the wind.

Every muscle in me went on high alert. Even Liam appeared ready to pounce. Bo, on the other hand, barked.

"Quinn." Chase's voice was soft. "It's only a party. Adults will be there. We can hang out. Nothing more."

The guy had me believing his story.

She backed away from him slightly, causing him to let go of her hair. "Can I think about it?"

Chase smiled. "Sure. Don't wait too long. My mom needs a head count."

"I'll g-give you my answer at school tomorrow," she said rather shyly.

Chase sighed, glancing at Liam and me as though he were about to do something that would incite us.

I held my breath because if he so much as kissed her, I might get fired before I even started my new job.

He patted Bo on the head. "Great. See you tomorrow." He waltzed to his car with his chest puffed out. Silence as thick as fog on a humid Southern night weaved around us until Chase was gone.

Liam growled. "Are you nuts, Quinn? He's up to something."

She shoved the invitation into the back pocket of her jeans. "So is it true that no boy has even approached me until now because of you and Carter? Never mind. I know the answer." Then she jabbed a finger into Liam's chest. "I can handle myself. Besides, it's not like Chase would try anything stupid with adults around."

Liam huffed. "Come, Bo." He stalked off with Bo trotting after him.

I wanted to believe her last line. But given that Chase and Tessa were kin, and Tessa had it out for Quinn, my money was on Chase doing something to hurt Quinn. For that, I probably should go to the party.

A car passed on the country road as Quinn and I stood in silence.

"Are you going to the Stevenses' party?" Quinn finally asked. "I saw Tessa give you an invitation."

It was on the tip of my tongue to ask her if she wanted me to go, but I was afraid she would say no. I wasn't afraid of much except horses and heights, yet I was standing in front of a girl who was making my insides go haywire, especially the more her cherry scent wafted around me.

"I don't do parties." *Liar. You went to a couple of your friends' parties in the ninth grade.*

She looked in all directions except at me.

"Quinn," Liam called. "Dad needs you down in the barn. Why don't you take Maiken and show him around?"

"Come on," she said. "I-I'll introduce you to my prize possession."

I stabbed a thumb at my car. "I should go. I have a lot of school-work to catch up on." It wasn't that I didn't want to spend time with Quinn. I wasn't sure I was ready to be around horses if that was what she'd meant by prize possession. I mean, a barn had horses in it.

Stop being such a pansy. If you're going to work here, then get used to animals.

She gave me a sad smile. "I'll see you at school, then." She started for a winding cement path with rolling hills on both sides.

My heart flipped out of control. The last thing I wanted was to make Quinn sad, so I jogged up to her.

Chapter 11

Quinn

I puffed out my cheeks, almost dizzy that Chase of all people had asked me to his party. He was handsome, but looks weren't everything. He'd sounded sincere and had even apologized, which was startling. Still, Chase could be up to something, but I didn't get that vibe. Maybe I was blinded by his sweet tone, and he'd been brave to ask me out in front of my brother, the same person who was responsible for making sure no boy in school asked me out. That told me Chase really liked me. Yet a little voice in the back of my head was telling me to tread lightly. After all, he was kin to my arch nemesis.

"So are you going to accept Chase's invitation?" Maiken asked as we headed to the barn.

For a split second, I thought I heard a tinge of jealousy in his tone, but I quickly erased that notion. No boy had ever been jealous over me. Besides, we hardly knew each other. He wouldn't ask me out anyway, not if my brothers had any say in the matter.

I wanted to stomp my feet like I'd done many times as a little girl when my brothers bossed me around. I loved that my brothers were protective, but they were not about to tell me whom I could and couldn't date.

I'd always wondered why boys hadn't approached me. Maybe it was time *I* asked a boy out. Momma wouldn't approve of that, though. She'd always said ladies didn't ask men out.

"Did you hear me, Quinn?" Maiken asked.

The strong scent of manure carried on the wind the closer we got to the barn, drawing me from my reverie. Or maybe Maiken's husky voice was what had gotten my attention. Either way, I disposed of thoughts of Chase's invitation, at least for the moment. I would have time later to think. Right then, I had a dreamy boy at my side, holding his nose as though he were about to gag.

One of horses nickered when we approached the barn door.

Maiken let go of his nose, and fear jumped off him as he looked inside.

"It's just Apple. She smells me. I'll introduce you." I went in, but Maiken didn't. I held back a giggle since it wasn't proper to ridicule him. People had fears of all kinds. I was afraid of snakes. We had plenty of garden snakes around the farm, yet I could never get used to them slithering by me or making me scream anytime one came out of nowhere.

"Did you know that horses have eight basic sounds they convey? One is the greeting nicker, which Apple is doing. She does it anytime people walk in, especially me. I promise Apple is not going to hurt you." I held out my hand. I wasn't spewing facts because I was nervous but to help him understand and hopefully ease his tension.

He rolled his shoulders back. "I'm not afraid."

Baloney!

Dad called my name.

I tossed a look over my shoulder. Stalls lined both sides of the barn with horses barricaded behind wrought-iron bars. Dad had remodeled the barn two years ago when we took in some rescue horses from a farm upstate that had been leveled by fire. We'd expected the owners to eventually retrieve their property, but they'd asked Dad if he wanted to keep the horses after they decided to move west.

Dad held a bale of hay outside one of the stalls. "Quinn, you have chores before it gets late, and Apple needs her blanket for the night."

Before I could move or speak, Maiken was at my side. "I'll help."

I was surprised at his sudden eagerness. Maybe Maiken wanted to prove something to my dad... or me. Yet the moment he'd crossed into the barn, he froze and his skin paled.

"There are a lot of horses in here," Maiken said to no one in particular.

"Son," Dad said to Maiken. "We could use some help."

Carter emerged from a stall midway down. "The horses need their water containers filled. Grab the hose." He pointed to a wall outside of Apple's stall. "Start filling each stall with fresh water." Bossy Carter spoke to Maiken as though Maiken had worked on a farm all his life like Carter.

Maiken audibly swallowed. "You want me to go inside the stalls?"

Dad and Carter swapped a confused look.

"I'll help him," I said.

Dad and Carter resumed their chores.

I snatched the hose, turned on the nozzle, then filled Apple's bucket, which was clamped to the wrought-iron bars and could be filled from outside the stall easily.

Color returned to Maiken's cheeks. "Oh. That's not hard."

"Do you not like horses?"

Apple came closer to me, and Maiken inched away, stiff and dazed.

"She's sweet and won't hurt you." I planted two hands on Maiken's back and nudged him closer to Apple.

He didn't budge. The boy was a wall of muscle. I tittered more out of nerves because I was actually touching the boy who was making my mouth dry and my stomach quiver.

"Okay," Maiken said. "I am afraid of horses. There, I said it."

I circled around him. "I promise you, none of the horses in here will hurt you." I rushed over to a small table near where the hose had been and grabbed an apple from the box. "If you feed this to Apple, she will be your best animal friend."

His face contorted. "I'd rather not."

I shrugged. "Another time, then." I wasn't about to push him. He had to come around on his own. So I fed her the apple then ducked into her stall and set her blanket on her back. We had heaters in the barn, but that night, the temp was supposed to drop well below zero. "Did you know that horses can create insulating air pockets to keep them warm?" I petted Apple. "But it's going to be super cold tonight, girl," I said to my prize horse. She wasn't one we took to horse shows, but I did ride her at least once a week to give her some much-needed exercise.

Maiken had his hands in his coat pockets. "You really are full of facts."

He had no idea.

I came out of Apple's stall. "We should finish filling the rest of the buckets."

Maiken helped but didn't get too close to the stalls. After we were done and the horses were all tucked in for the night, I walked Maiken back to his car.

"A horse almost bit off my finger when I was little," Maiken said.

"Really? That almost happened to me too."

He stopped halfway between the barn and the farm store. "And you're not afraid of them?"

"Not at all. Were you trying to feed the horse?" That had happened to me when I was little before Daddy taught me about horses.

As he nodded, his blue eyes twinkled in the landscape lights along the path. "My dad's buddy had a horse, and I ran up to it, excited to feed him some carrots. Then at the last second as the horse was chomping away on the carrot, he almost bit my fingers. Thankfully, I pulled away quickly. I noticed you held out your palm with the apple on top of it."

"You should always put the food in your palm so your fingers won't get in the way. Even then, it's not guaranteed a horse won't bite a finger. My dad doesn't like me hand-feeding the horses, even Apple."

We resumed walking.

"So earlier today when we were leaving the gym, did I say something to upset you?" Maiken asked. "If I did, I'm sorry."

That afternoon seemed eons away already. Still, I hadn't forgotten that he'd said I was different. I debated whether to tell him that he'd hit a nerve because when the rumors had gone around school that I was easy, boys would approach me with that line.

But I was beginning to realize that Maiken wasn't like those boys, and surprisingly, neither was Chase Stevens. *Wow!* For a girl who never got a second glance from a boy, I'd hit the jackpot in one day. Chase had asked me out and told me he liked me. Maiken hadn't asked me out, but he was kind and friendly to me, which was refreshing, exciting, and scary all at the same time—scary because I felt Maiken could be the boy to break my heart.

Nevertheless, I said, "You didn't upset me." I didn't want to make a big thing about it, and he seemed genuine and sincere.

He gave me a warm smile as we stood near his Suburban. An awkward and quiet moment stretched between us. He looked around. I checked the hut, which resembled a very large wooden box with a window opening that had been boarded up for the night.

"So are you going to say yes to Chase's invitation?" he asked.

I tucked my hands into my sweatshirt. "I don't know." For the last two years, I'd always wished I would get an invite or that Momma and Daddy would receive one and I could tag along. I'd always heard how entertaining the Stevenses' holiday galas were with nifty finger foods, desserts, and the white-elephant game in which everyone brought a gift and was given a number. The person with number one picked any gift from among the partygoers. Then the person with number two could pick the gift from the first person or choose a gift from anyone else. The process continued until the last person in the sequence, who was the real winner, chose any gift in the room.

Food and games weren't reasons to say yes to Chase, and neither were my desire to put on a pretty dress, do my hair, or the fact that a boy had finally asked me out. Sure, Chase was cute, but I'd never considered him boyfriend material. If I did say yes, I wanted to be sure I liked him. At the moment, I wasn't sure how I felt about him.

"So you were on the court today. Does that mean you're playing for the team now?"

He lifted a jacket-covered shoulder. "I didn't get a chance to talk to

S.B. ALEXANDER

Coach Dean. I'm not real sure yet." He lightly touched my cheek. "The area around your eyes isn't so dark."

Thoughts of basketball, holiday parties, and Chase went poof into the night as goose bumps fired along my arms, especially when Maiken traced the area under my eye. His finger was rough, yet his touch was soft.

I swore I was a second away from lifting up on my toes and kissing his perfect lips. At that thought, my nerves started to sing. "D-did you know that electrical energy can be transformed into h-heat energy?"

One side of his mouth curled as his gaze traveled down to my lips. "Is that so? Does that fact have something to do with your black eyes?"

Heat stung my cheeks despite the frigid temperature. "No. I m-masked my bruises with makeup."

Someone cleared his throat.

Maiken jumped back as if I had some kind of disease. My feet were frozen to the gravel.

Carter stalked up, breathing fire. "What are you doing? Are you seriously touching my sister? Is that why you took the job? To get close to her?"

I pursed my lips, narrowed my eyes, and closed my hands into fists. I swore I would kill my brother if he so much as hurt Maiken.

Maiken raised his hands. "What?"

Carter got in his face. "Let's get something straight. My sister is off-limits. Do you understand?"

I wanted to scream. Instead, I latched on to Carter's tense bicep. "Stop it."

"We were just talking," Maiken said.

Carter eased back but not that far from Maiken. "Mom is looking for you, Quinn,"

Maiken rushed over to the driver's side door of his car. "I've got to get home."

Before I knew what was happening, Maiken was driving away.

"He's not right for you," Carter said. "And you're not dating."

I laughed, but it was an evil and nervous laugh. "You're not my

76

father, and you sure don't get to pick the boys I talk to or date for that matter."

He grinned. I knew that grin. It was one that said I was wrong. "And you're not going to the Stevenses' party with Chase either."

I snarled. I was going to kill Liam for tattling. I stomped away. "We'll see about that."

Carter didn't react. He never did unless it was to defend my honor or protect me. But protection was keeping me safe, not telling me whom I could or couldn't date.

Chapter 12

Maiken

School had been canceled due to another snowstorm that had barreled in overnight. My younger siblings had had a blast playing in the snow and building a snowman. I'd even enjoyed having a snowball fight with Ethan and Marcus.

I sauntered into Coach Dean's office. "You wanted to see me?"

He lifted his gaze from his computer screen.

Even though school was out, Coach hadn't canceled practice that afternoon. By the time I'd arrived at the gym, the roads were clear and the sun was shining. The temperature, however, was different a story. I swore my lips had frozen from the car to the sports complex.

Coach waved a hand toward an armless chair in front of his desk. "Have a seat."

I did as I was told. I had an inkling why I was in his office. He and I were supposed to talk after practice the day before, but he'd had to run to an appointment.

"I liked what I saw from you on the court yesterday, but I have concerns."

I did as well. The only reason I'd practiced with the team was to taunt Chase. Yet shooting the ball, passing the ball, hearing the squeak of my basketball shoes on the wood floor, and the atmosphere of the gym had infused me with elation and excitement. I missed the game. It had been months since I had a ball in my hands.

The questions remained, though. Could I play, work, and study? Would I have time to take care of my family? I'd tossed and turned all night, searching for answers to those questions among other things.

Basketball season was only four months long with two or three games per week. Plus, I had to factor in practice, which was every day we didn't have a game. So I would only have time at night and on weekends to work and study.

What are you worried about? You've played and studied before.

But now I have a job. A job that ends right before Christmas.

So you shouldn't factor that in.

I was leaning toward playing. Whether I had a job or my mom moved the entire family back to the South, basketball was my drug. I needed the game more than Coach needed a player.

Wrinkles rimmed his brown eyes. "It seems you and Chase have a problem with each other. I'm sure you know, son, that chemistry among the team is what wins games. If you boys aren't in sync, then we don't stand a chance at making it to the playoffs. So if you want the spot of shooting guard, then it's yours. But I'm giving you one warning. If you and Chase display any animosity on the court, then you're off the team. Is that understood?"

I chewed the inside of my cheek. "Isn't Chase a shooting guard?" I'd learned that yesterday from Chase when he'd said, "You're not taking my position."

Considering there was only one shooting-guard position on a team, I was sure he wouldn't go down without a fight.

Coach leaned back in his chair. "I'm making some changes."

"Does Chase know this?" Even if he did, it wouldn't change how upset he was going to be. "With all due respect, sir, I'm not playing basketball." I would be off the team before I even played anyway. I wasn't about to let Chase spit fire at me without retaliating. My dad had always taught me to stick up for myself.

Coach popped forward and leaned his elbows on his desk. "Why not? I'll handle Chase."

A nervous laugh erupted from me. "It wouldn't matter. You could talk to him until the cows come home. And the one warning you're giving me is already moot before I even walk out of your office." Sure, I could promise him I would be a model player, but I would be lying. Regardless of basketball, Chase and I would face off. It was just a matter of time.

What I was sure about was that Quinn wasn't going to Chase's party without me. I'd thought about her too as I'd stared at the popcorn ceiling from my bed during the night. I'd had the urge to kiss her before I'd gotten into my car the evening before. Hell, I had many urges that had nothing to do with playing basketball and everything to do with the girl with butterscotch hair.

Despite my manly cravings, Chase had an ulterior motive. I wasn't talking about him kissing her either. He was brewing up something, and no way would I let Quinn be the brunt of his antics. After all, he was the brother to Quinn's number-one enemy.

Besides, she was my girl. I'd never had a girlfriend. I'd always left the sighing, the long nights texting on the phone, and the dating to my brother Ethan. He was the ladies' man. Yet there I was silently staking claim to a girl with soft skin, big brown eyes, and a shyness that twisted me and made me feel alive.

You'll have to get through her brother Carter. I could've kicked my own butt for not defending myself against the big, scary brother. Quinn probably thought I was frightened out of my mind, but the only reason I'd taken off faster than the roadrunner was for the simple reason that Carter was my employer in a roundabout way. I didn't want to ruin a job before it even started.

Coach scrubbed a hand over his jaw, considering me. He probably knew I was right and didn't have anything else to say.

I didn't either. I'd come to his office prepared to play, but it was time to grab a bite before I started my shift at the farm.

Holding out my hand, I rose. "Thanks for letting me practice yesterday."

Footsteps clobbered in the hall, drawing Coach's attention to the door.

Chase appeared, and that was definitely my cue to leave. "Stevens," I said, trying to be polite.

His nostrils flared.

I could feel mine doing the same.

We were like two bulls in an arena, about to face off. I'd had run-ins with other boys at previous schools I'd attended, but there was something about Chase that went deep into my bones and made me want to wipe the smug look off his pimpled face. Or maybe my anger was directed more at the death of my dad. I'd been on edge since his funeral, and as the days went by, I thought time would heal my pain and sorrow. But I was far from healing, maybe because I hadn't had time to grieve. I'd been so dedicated to my siblings, my mom, and making sure they were okay, that I'd left little time for myself.

"Boys," Coach said at my back.

He didn't need to say anymore. I bumped Chase's shoulder as I marched out and into the bitter cold, which was a welcome relief from the heated confines of the school.

Within twenty minutes, I was sitting in the driveway at home, staring at the basketball hoop over the garage. I wished beyond anything my dad was there. He was the one person I could talk to. Sure, I could talk to my mom, and she would give me her advice, but she would sugarcoat her words. I loved her for it, but Dad hadn't minced words. I didn't want to burden Mom with my problems either, which didn't all revolve around Chase.

I was behind in math and English, although I'd never had stellar grades. That feat went to my sister Emma. Still, my mind was ten million miles away.

An engine whirred, pulling me from my trance. A tractor came around from the side of the garage. Kade waved as he parked the John Deere in front of one of the bay doors then hopped down. He'd told me I could talk to him if I needed to. Maybe he would be a good sounding board.

I abandoned the warm car. "Are you clearing the backyard?"

He pressed a remote, and one of the six bay doors opened. "Just clearing a path down to the boathouse, or rather funhouse as Lacey likes to call it, although it's just an apartment these days."

Since we'd arrived, the snow had prevented us from exploring more of the property, and Mom didn't want us going down to the lake, or I should say she didn't want the younger kids to venture anywhere near the ice-covered water without supervision. I knew about the boathouse, but no one had mentioned that it was an apartment, which started me thinking.

Kade peeled off his gloves. "I've got a repairman coming out tomorrow to fix the heater in the apartment."

It wasn't that the house seemed crowded, but it would be nice to have a place to go and think and maybe study. "You think I could use it when the heater is fixed? I wouldn't mind hanging out there."

He grinned as though he'd done that very thing when he were a teenager. "I don't see why not. You can help me clean it out, and then we can set it up as a game room like it used to be when I was younger." He glanced at his watch. "I thought you were at basketball practice."

"Coach gave me an impossible goal. So I decided not to play."

The garage had two cars in the middle two stalls. On the far side sat a boxing ring that piqued my interest. I wondered if my brother Marcus knew about that. He was the one who loved boxing. My brothers and I loved all sports, but each of us had a favorite. While my love for basketball trumped the other sports, Jasper was into football, Ethan was into baseball, and Marcus had two loves—boxing and rugby. Harlan was too enamored with lizards and nature to have an interest in a sport, but I was sure he would one day.

Kade removed his knit hat and grabbed the basketball that was sitting on a rolling cart near the side door and tossed me the ball.

The minute the ball was in my hands, a calming effect washed over me. Suddenly, I was transported back to our former home in Texas when my dad would shoot hoops with me. I distinctly remembered the hot summer sun beating down as Dad blocked me when I went in for a layup. He'd played in high school and had been fortunate to get accepted to UCLA, where he'd played shooting guard. His dreams had died suddenly when he'd broken his ankle. After that, his game had never been the same.

Kade clapped a hand on my shoulder. "Let's see what you got." He tipped his head at the hoop.

"Do you play?" Aside from my father, I hadn't been aware of anyone in our family who played the game.

He ran a hand through his honey-colored hair, which I realized was almost the same color as Quinn's.

Suddenly, images of her were dancing through my head—her smile, the way she looked at me but quickly shied away, and above all else, the way her hand felt in mine—so soft and delicate.

"The family has an occasional pickup game on Sundays sometimes." Kade's voice penetrated through my reverie.

I bounced the ball once then twice before I shot it. It scored the rim and landed near Kade, who stood near the net.

He tossed it back to me. "So Coach gave you a goal?"

I nodded as I positioned myself to shoot again. "Do you know Chase Stevens?"

"I know the family. I can't say I know the kids well. Let me guess. You two don't get along?"

When the ball left my hand, I shrugged. "Something like that." That time, the ball swished through the net.

Kade and I got into a routine with him passing the ball back to me and me shooting. The more the ball swished through the hoop, the more I wanted to play the game.

After ten minutes, Kade came over and handed me the ball. "Can I give you some advice?"

I wanted to shout yes. But instead, I dipped my head.

"Don't let anyone get in the way of what you want. Lacey had a problem back in high school with the captain of the baseball team." He grinned. "She didn't let him get the best of her. If you want to play, then play. If Chase gives you trouble, then deal with it. The question is do you want to play ball? Because if you want to as badly as I think you do, then you wouldn't let anything or anyone stop you."

I swore I was listening to my dad, and because of that, tears threatened. "I do want to play. I also want to help my mom out financially. I know what I make isn't going to support a family of nine. But if I can make enough for gas and to buy lunch at school, that would be one less burden on her."

He smiled so wide. "Maiken, you remind me of me when I was your age." Then he lost his smile. "So work a part-time job. Working doesn't mean you have to give up basketball. Besides, Mr. Thompson's son plays ball. So I'm sure Mr. Thompson will be very accommodating to your schedule."

I tucked the ball underneath my arm. "What about Chase?"

"You'll figure out how to handle him."

"Even if he and I get into a brawl?" It wasn't even a matter of *if* but *when,* especially if he so much as touched Quinn.

Kade started for the garage. "Talk to Chase."

I followed then placed the ball back on the cart. "Is that what you and your brothers did back in high school? Talk, I mean, to your enemies?"

Jerking his head at me, he snatched a shovel that was hanging on the wall. "What my brothers and I went through shouldn't have gotten as far as it did. Find a common ground. Find a way to at least be civil to Chase and still play basketball."

I refrained from rolling my eyes. His advice was an impossible feat. Chase wouldn't listen to anything I had to say.

Chapter 13

Quinn

Since school had been canceled, Momma put me to work in the farm store shortly after lunch while she spent the afternoon taking care of errands. I'd called Celia to join me so we could hang out. We were far from busy. Snow always made people hibernate. I wasn't complaining, though. It gave Celia and me time to rekindle our friendship.

She and I sat on stools behind the register, chatting and messing with our phones.

"I'm so glad we're friends again," Celia said.

"Ditto, bestie. If you ever have any notion of ditching me again for Tessa, I just might commit a crime," I teased, but underneath I was a tad serious. Celia and I had been close since elementary school, and I would've been more devastated the second time around, although I didn't think she would ditch me again.

"Are you going to say yes to Chase's invitation?" Celia asked.

For the last couple of hours, we'd talked nonstop about the Stevenses' party. Her mom had secured the contract to cater the lavish event.

I set my phone down on the counter underneath the window. I'd thought about his invitation, but honestly, my mind had been more occupied with Maiken. I sighed, touching the area under my eyes, thinking back to the connection we'd had until Carter ruined every-thing. "I still look like a raccoon. Don't I?"

Celia snorted. "With the makeup, you really can't tell all that much."

"Pfft. You're just trying to make me feel better."

"Isn't that what besties do? Now back to Chase."

"Argh." I was supposed to give him my answer at school that morning, so I was relieved for the moment that I had another day to think about it. I really didn't need to, though. Sure, I was flattered that he'd confessed to liking me since grade school. I was also shocked that he'd been man enough to admit as much with Liam and Maiken present. Yet Chase didn't touch my heart like Maiken did. The minute I'd laid eyes on Maiken, my heart had gone haywire. With Chase, my heart didn't even flutter.

"As much as I want to go to the party, my answer is no. I don't want to lead him on."

Celia looked up from her phone. "Smart. I don't think boys know how to be friends, or at least I don't get that vibe from Chase." She reached over and placed her hand on my thigh. "It's an adult party anyway. They're boring."

She was right. But I loved Christmas parties and decorations and an atmosphere where everyone was filled with cheer. Frankly, I was tired of being the only one in town who'd never gotten an invite.

Her pink lips split into a smile. "After last night and the time you spent with Maiken, maybe he'll ask you out on a date. You did say you thought he was jealous of Chase when Chase gave you the invitation."

I clucked my tongue. "After last night, Maiken will never ask me out. Carter will make sure of that."

"Your brothers are—"

I held up my hand. "Don't say it. I know they're the reason no boy has approached me in a serious way. Now Maiken probably won't talk to me."

"Yet Chase stood up to Liam, right?" she asked.

"Liam isn't as scary as Carter," I added. "And Liam follows Carter's lead most of the time."

She tucked her phone in the back pocket of her jeans. "So Chase was sweet, huh?"

"He wasn't the Chase I knew." He'd always been standoffish. But I knew why now—my brothers. "We've been talking about me. Tell me what you and Liam were arguing about outside the gym yesterday."

She gnawed on her lip. "I had every intention of apologizing to him for coming on too strong, but instead, I asked him to help my mom and me with the catering for the Stevenses' party. He took that as a date and flat out said no. He just doesn't want anything to do with me."

I hated to see her sad. I would say something to Liam, but I was by far not an expert on boys. On occasion, I had overheard Carter and Liam talking about girls. Carter believed that girls shouldn't chase boys. Momma had taught her children that girls had a place and so did boys. Daddy agreed. Carter and Liam always talked about that very thing. They didn't like when girls hung all over them or were forward and asked them out.

"Forward girls are trouble," Daddy had said, as had my granny.

I hopped off the stool. "Can I tell you something?" I might as well give her the inside scoop on Liam. Maybe that would help.

Her espresso eyes filled with intrigue. "Of course."

I leaned against the counter. "Let him come to you. He's been taught that girls don't ask boys out." If he liked Celia, and I didn't know if he did, then he would take the lead when he was ready.

She pouted. "I might be waiting a long time."

Join the club. I could be waiting forever for Maiken to make the first move.

The bell on the door dinged. *Finally, a customer.* Momma would be happy about that. But when I turned, the customer was actually Momma. She stomped her feet to shake off the snow on her boots. "Business is slow, I see. Celia, if you need to go and help your mom, I'll take it from here with Quinn."

"No, ma'am. My mom closed the bakery early. She and one of her employees had to go shopping for supplies for the Stevenses' party."

Momma smoothed a hand over her hair to tame the wispy strands. "Speaking of the party, Mrs. Stevens called." She set her brown gaze on me. "She wants to know if you're going, Quinn. Apparently, her son asked you to go with him? When were you going to tell me?" Hurt peppered her tone.

I hadn't had a chance to see Momma since she'd left early to meet Mrs. Maxwell for breakfast and then run errands. "Chase stopped by last night and asked me. You were gone when I got up this morning." I'd gone straight to my room after Maiken had left last night thanks in part to Carter, who had irritated me.

Momma set her purse on the counter near the register. "And you said?"

"I told him I wanted to think about it. I don't like him as a boyfriend."

"Then tell him that," Momma said.

Celia rose and rested her elbows on the counter next to me. "I think Quinn should go with Maiken."

Momma lifted an eyebrow. "Is he going? Eleanor was invited." Momma's voice hitched. "I saw you two walking from the barn last night. You would like for Maiken to be your date. Wouldn't you?"

"Tessa asked him to go. But he told me he doesn't do parties. Besides, it's not his party to invite me to."

Momma drilled her dark-brown eyes into me. "You didn't answer my question."

"Yes, ma'am. I would rather go out with Maiken."

She came around the counter. "Eleanor says Maiken is going through a rough time right now with the death of his father. Just be patient."

That was easier said than done when all I wanted to do was kiss the boy who was slowly stealing my heart.

Chapter 14

Maiken

The job wasn't hard in the least. A customer picked a tree, then I baled the tree in plastic netting and loaded it in or on top of their vehicle. Since starting my shift, I'd helped five customers, talked to Mr. Thompson, kept watching for Quinn to show up, and was waiting for Liam to get back from practice. He was over an hour late. My shift had started at five, and it was well past six.

When I asked Mr. Thompson when Liam would arrive, he said Liam wasn't working that night. *Darn.* I was dying to pick Liam's brain about practice. When I'd left Coach's office, Chase had been walking in. I was curious if Coach had had the same conversation with Chase that he'd had with me or if Chase had talked smack on the court about me not playing.

In between helping customers, I thought about my conversation with Kade. I shouldn't let Chase or anyone dictate what I did. Kade was right when he'd said my mom was a strong woman. She'd always had a good grasp on the family as the matriarch, and she still did even though my dad had passed, but I could tell she was wearing a cloak to mask her sorrow. She wasn't her happy self, and I was sure most of my brothers and sisters could see that.

Regardless of my mom, maybe I should talk to Chase in an attempt to appeal to his softer side. Better yet, I could play point guard instead of shooting guard. I didn't like that I would fill Alex's position. I didn't want to be judged against a star athlete, although I'd filled positions of former star players who had graduated at the other schools I'd attended. The operative word was graduated. Alex died. I felt that people would give me trouble if I didn't live up to Alex's talent. Then again, I didn't know if Alex was talented or not, which didn't matter. Someone had to fill his shoes.

The thing was I wasn't a point guard. I wasn't the player to orchestrate the offense. I wasn't the player with exceptional ball-handling skills. I was the player who scored points. *No matter what you do, Chase isn't going to like you.* I was sure of that.

A bitter-cold wind whipped around. Mr. Thompson fixed his knit hat so it covered his ears. "Temps are supposed to drop below zero tonight."

I popped up and rubbed my hands over the fire flickering out of a metal drum. If it got any colder, I swore my lips would freeze together.

Mr. Thompson joined me, buttoning his flannel shirt.

I blew into my hands. "Do you get used to the cold?" I imagined he did since he wasn't wearing a jacket.

"Not really, but when you're moving as much as I do throughout the day with all the things we have to do on the farm, then you keep warm."

We both stared at the flames, rubbing our hands over the fire when a *clip, clop, clip, clop* made Mr. Thompson jerk up his head. It took me a minute to realize that someone was riding a horse.

I stiffened. Mr. Thompson darted to the edge of the road. A second later, the horse came into view, and when I dragged my gaze up to the rider, my jaw dropped.

Quinn looked like a queen or a goddess with her long hair draped around her. A smile appeared on her rosy face, and I wished I could capture her expression. I wanted to put it into my mom's scrapbook so I could cherish it forever. A headlamp beamed down from her forehead. On anyone else, the lamp would look odd, but not on her.

The horse I suspected was Apple made a sound as Mr. Thompson ran a hand down its neck. "You shouldn't be out on the road in the dark, young lady. How many times have I told you that?"

Quinn's smile faded as she hopped off like an expert rider, which I was sure she was since she'd grown up around horses. "I took Apple out before it got dark, and we got sidetracked. Sorry, Daddy." She rose on her toes and kissed him on the cheek.

Since Mr. Thompson's back was to me, I couldn't see his expression, but his body seemed to deflate. The exchange between father and daughter reminded me of how my sisters had had Dad wrapped around their fingers.

Mr. Thompson grabbed Apple's reins. "I'll take her to the barn. Stay with Maiken in case he needs help with the register."

Sure, this was my first job, but the register wasn't hard at all. All I had to do was press a button, and the drawer would open.

Quinn gave me one of her shy grins. My stomach did a wild dance until headlights brightened the dark road. Quinn abandoned me for the SUV that slowed until the driver pulled into the lot. And it wasn't just any driver. Chase Stevens was behind the wheel. It figured he would be the one to interrupt Quinn and me.

At that moment, anger, hot and bright, burned a path through me. Or maybe the flames from the fire were licking my hands. I bit my lip, willing myself to keep calm. *Mr. Thompson doesn't want trouble. Remember?* I had to be on best behavior. *You wanted to talk to Chase anyway. So talk to him.*

Chase climbed out, dressed in jeans and a T-shirt. His hair was wet as though he'd rushed out of the shower to get over to the farm.

I willed his hair to freeze to his head, even more so when he sauntered up to Quinn. That was my cue to kick my butt into gear and rescue my girl.

Mr. Thompson walked Apple into the parking lot. "Chase, what brings you by?"

Quinn glided up to her dad and Chase.

Apple's tail swung back and forth.

I joined them, staying away from Apple but keeping an eye on the horse just in case. I knew I was being weird and that Apple wouldn't hurt me, but that fear of horses I had embedded in me wasn't exactly waning much.

Quinn must've noticed when she skirted Chase to stand beside me.

A laugh resonated in my head. I should have been the one protecting her from the likes of Chase.

Chase held out his hand to Apple. "Hey, girl." Then he petted the area around her neck. "Sir, I'm here to talk to Quinn."

Quinn frowned at me.

My stomach took a nosedive. She was going to say yes to his invitation.

What the hell?

Mr. Thompson guided Apple toward the path that led down to the barn. "Make it quick, Chase. Quinn has chores to do still."

A truck wheeled into the lot before a man in his forties got out and started looking at the trees under the lighted pergola.

Mr. Thompson returned, leaving Apple tied to the fence. Reluctantly, I abandoned Quinn and Chase and rushed to help the customer. I had a job to do, even though I didn't want to leave Quinn with Chase. I also wanted to show Mr. Thompson I could handle things.

"Can I help you find a particular tree?" I asked.

The middle-aged man with a thick beard browsed the variety of short, tall, skinny, and fat trees. "Just looking right now."

I eyed Mr. Thompson, who watched me intently. Then I tossed a look in Quinn's direction. Chase was grinning at her as though he were truly in love with her.

Nausea settled heavily in my stomach at the notion that he could very well be in love with her. However, I wasn't sure if I believed he didn't have an ulterior motive to bully her in some way, especially after witnessing his crass interaction with her at school the day before. Sometimes boys tried not to show how they really felt. At least that was something my mom had said a time or two to Emma.

Quinn and Chase walked to the back of his SUV.

Mr. Thompson shoved his hands in his jeans pockets, watching his daughter. Maybe he stayed because of Quinn and not me.

"I'll take this one," the customer said.

I heard him but didn't rush to help like I was supposed to.

Mr. Thompson cleared his throat. "Maiken?"

At his deep, commanding tone, I snapped to and helped the man, making quick work of baling the tree. Meanwhile, the customer moseyed over to Mr. Thompson with his wallet, ready to pay.

I tried to listen to Quinn and Chase's conversation, but it was useless since the baler was near the hut and a good distance away from Chase's truck. After the tree was loaded and the customer drove away, I went over to stand by the fire while Mr. Thompson fiddled with the register. The horse seemed to be happy just hanging out not far from me. But Apple could've trotted over to me, and I wouldn't have cared. My only focus was keeping an eye on Chase and Quinn, who were now clear in my view.

Quinn listened intently as he talked. Then he slipped his hand in hers. She didn't pull away or move at all.

I ground my back teeth together. *Take a breath. Don't do anything you'll regret. You're at your job, your first job at that, and your boss is present.*

Chase lowered his head to whisper in her ear.

The fire crackled, or maybe it was one of my teeth cracking.

Chase tucked strands of Quinn's hair behind her ear.

I saw stars and my fist in Chase's face. All sense of where I was vaporized as I stalked over to the happy couple with my hands clenched so tightly that my stubby nails pierced the skin on my palms.

Chase and Quinn rounded their gazes on me. Quinn had fear swimming in her pretty amber eyes. Chase had excitement in his.

Again, as though she could protect me, or maybe Chase, Quinn slid in between us.

Chase snarled. "You got a problem, Maxwell?"

"Yeah. You."

S.B. ALEXANDER

Quinn was a head shorter than me, so it wasn't as if she was blocking my view of Chase's acne covered face.

Mr. Thompson ran over. "What's going on?"

"Nothing, Daddy," Quinn said in a rush.

Mr. Thompson's hand went around my bicep. "Doesn't look like nothing." His tone could've cut ice. "Son, I want you to sweep up the area around the baler. Chase, head on home."

Chase breathed fire.

Quinn's small hands landed on my abs. "Do as my father says." There was no stuttering whatsoever on her part.

If it weren't for her touch or her singsong voice, I probably would've made darn sure that Chase had a broken nose before he got into his car.

I sighed heavily before I marched over to the hut, snatched the broom, and did as I was told. Quinn followed me as Mr. Thompson said something to Chase that I couldn't hear. Chase shook Mr. Thompson's hand before driving off.

I swept as though I were trying to dig a hole to bury the baler. *What is wrong with me?* I was letting some dude who I barely knew get under my skin. *You're jealous.* If that was what jealousy felt like, then I didn't want any part of dating or liking a girl. I needed to go back to thinking girls were all created equal. At least then I could focus on working and not losing my job or feeling as though I was a second away from losing my shit.

Once the SUV's engine faded, Mr. Thompson marched up to me with pursed lips and that mean look I was becoming accustomed to. "What did I tell you about trouble?"

Quinn jumped to my defense. "Daddy, he was only trying to protect me like Carter and Liam."

So true. Yet my intentions weren't brotherly. *She's my girl, and no one touches her.* She didn't know that. *No one but you does.*

Her dad let out a laugh that said he believed that was a lie. "Seems to me you're jealous, son. Or you have a beef with a boy whose position you're trying to steal on the basketball team."

94

I stopped sweeping, and my face contorted. "Is that what he told you?"

So many swear words filled my head and were on the tip of my tongue. To think I had wanted to play nice with Chase. *Not anymore.*

Quinn's jaw was on the tips of her boots.

Mr. Thompson considered his daughter. "So Chase invited you to the Stevenses' holiday party?" He not only seemed surprised, but he didn't sound happy at all.

Quinn held her bottom lip hostage, looking at her feet and anywhere else but at her dad or me, and nodded.

From the looks of Chase and Quinn's exchange, I would bet she'd said yes, and for that, I screamed the word *fuck* to myself.

Her dad clutched the back of his neck. "Quinn, take Apple back to the barn. We'll talk about the party later."

She barely gave me a passing glance as she obeyed her father.

I wanted to ask her if she'd said yes but not with her father present. He already thought I was jealous. *So what's the harm?* More humiliation. I would get a chance the next day when I could get Quinn alone. Right then, I had to finish sweeping and doing my job, not pine over my boss's daughter, especially in front of my boss.

Quinn and Apple clobbered down the path.

Mr. Thompson wagged a finger at me. "Something like that happens again, I will not only fire you, but I'll make darn sure that none of the Maxwells ever step foot on this farm. Are we clear?"

"Yes, sir."

It wasn't his threat of firing me that had me agreeing. My aunt Eleanor would be devastated if she couldn't shop in the farm store or visit Mrs. Thompson, her best friend. I wasn't the type to care what people thought of me, but I did respect my family and would never hurt them. On top of all that, my mom would be so disappointed in me, and that would gut me.

"Good." He disappeared into the hut.

I resumed sweeping, thinking of how funny it was that I'd been invited to a party by Quinn's enemy and she'd been invited by mine.

Hell if I was going, though. But the comedy of it all was quickly replaced by the anger welling up inside me at how Chase had lied to Mr. Thompson. Then again, I shouldn't have been surprised. As I dumped dried pine needles into the trash can, I decided on one thing—I would play basketball, and not in any other position but shooting guard.

Chapter 15

Quinn

School resumed the next day, and I was a bundle of nerves as I waited for Maiken to show up. I yawned as I fished my math book out of my locker. I hadn't slept all that well, worrying about Maiken and how he was feeling after Daddy had reprimanded him. Between Daddy and Carter, Maiken would never talk to me again.

The hall wasn't as packed as it usually was in the mornings. I suspected that some kids were running late because of the roads. A light dusting had left the landscape with more snow, although not enough to cancel school again.

Celia wasn't around either. She'd texted me to let me know she would be late.

I was about to walk into math class when Tessa's voice trilled through the hall. I swore her voice had a nails-on-the-chalkboard effect. Her laugh was even more grating on the nerves.

Tessa flipped her shiny hair over her shoulder as she made a beeline for me with her breasts out, head up, and wearing that look of disgust that she only wore for me. Normally, I would run in the opposite direction, but I was curious if she knew Chase had asked me to the party. I imagined he'd told her since they were siblings.

She wrinkled her nose. "My mom told me a wild tale that you were coming to my party. I told her it couldn't be true, not a girl who works in pig shit all day and smells like one too."

I could feel my hand close into a fist while my other hand clutched tightly to the strap of my backpack. The need to erase her repugnant look was so strong that I had to press my hand to my leg.

Her dark eyes homed in on my clenched hand. "You want to punch me?" She sounded surprised, which she should have considering we'd never physically fought. I usually cowered when she spat venom.

I was shocking myself, but this was one instant in which I couldn't walk away. I was actually enjoying myself, even though I was a ball of nerves. I was dying to know how she felt about Chase inviting me.

"Did y-your m-mom—" *Jeepers, Quinn, stop stuttering.* I stood up straighter. This girl wasn't going to reduce me to nothing or make me feel as if I were pathetic anymore. *Okay, maybe my subconscious is braver than me.* "Did she tell you who invited me?"

"She mentioned you were going as one of Eleanor Maxwell's guests," Tessa said.

I reared back. Suddenly, I was majorly confused. Mrs. Stevens had told Momma that her son had asked me. So why hadn't she shared that with Tessa?

Lockers banged shut, snapping me out of my bewildered state.

Tessa inched closer, her minty breath breezing over me. "Is that not true?"

I hated to lie to her or anyone, but if I told her the truth, she wouldn't believe me. Then we would argue. The kids in the hall would egg us on and possibly convince Tessa to do something drastic like hit me.

Despite that, Chase had to have a good reason for not telling his sister he'd invited me. I mean, even Mrs. Stevens had lied.

"Why would your mom lie?" I asked. It was a great question.

She puckered her lips. "My mom doesn't lie."

"That's your answer, then." I left her standing in the hall as I scooted toward my AP math class before I said anything else. I didn't want to cause a ruckus.

I didn't get far before her nails dug into my arm. "Just because you know Mrs. Maxwell doesn't mean Maiken is going with you. I invited him. He's *my* date."

Now I knew why she was so edgy. She thought I would go with Maiken. Still, Tessa was making it more difficult for me to ignore her. Or maybe I had more confidence from knowing that two boys liked me. Maiken had never told me as much, but his jealousy was a good indication.

I tilted my head as I looked at her. "Does Maiken know that? He told me he doesn't do parties. So you should check with him. I know how you hate looking like a fool."

She gaped.

My work was done.

Walking into class, I gave myself several mental high fives for not stuttering. For the first time, I had rendered her speechless. *Chalk one up for Quinn Thompson, shy girl.*

The morning dragged by, and I was on alert for Maiken. But I had mostly advanced placement classes that he wasn't in. In addition, I'd also wanted to confront Chase. It boggled my mind why his mother would lie to her own daughter... unless she was protecting her son for some reason. Maybe Chase didn't want his sister to know he liked me.

The noise level in the cafeteria was at an all-time high when I walked in. Silverware clanked, students laughed, and chairs scraped along the tiled floor. Celia had texted me during my last class to meet her at our usual table in the far back of the cafeteria. Normally, that spot was quiet and out of the way of the craziness that happened at lunch.

I had my sights set on our table and didn't see the tall boy who popped out and into the aisle. It took me a minute to realize it was Maiken.

"Hey, there you are. I've been looking for you," Maiken said.

My belly swirled in delight at the handsome Maxwell who was rocking army boots, jeans, and a Kensington High sweatshirt. His hair was styled to perfection. James Dean came to mind only because I'd watched a movie or two of his while at Granny's house. She loved the handsome actor. In my opinion, James Dean's blue eyes were nothing compared to Maiken's. *Yum.*

I discarded the inappropriate thoughts and tried to focus on Maiken, whom I was actually surprised to see. I was sure he would stay away from me after Carter had almost torn his head off two nights ago and my dad had given him a stern warning the night before about causing trouble.

Maiken tucked his hands in the pocket of his sweatshirt. "I was wondering if we could feed the horses again after my shift is over tonight?"

I could feel the stares in the room riveted on Maiken and me, or maybe it was just my imagination. The only people who might have heard his question were the kids at the table I was standing next to. I braved a look to find Ethan Maxwell grinning as his brown eyes swam with mischief.

I opened my mouth to speak when Chase came out of nowhere. "Hey, Quinn. Do you want to sit with me?"

I was living in another universe in which I was the most popular girl in school.

Ha! Me? The most popular girl? That wasn't happening. I was shy and a nerd, and boys didn't ogle me.

Because of your brothers.

Maiken sneered at Chase. "I was talking to her. Don't be rude."

Chase puffed out his chest at Maiken. "We could finish what you started last night."

Maiken got in his face. "I would love to."

I tried to slip in between the two tall boys like I had the night before, which was becoming a habit.

Ethan charged to his brother's side, ready to fight off Chase. He was rather tall but not the height of Chase or Maiken, nor did he have broad shoulders like his brother. "Bro, let's go." Ethan placed a hand on his brother's chest, turning his back to Chase. "Don't you need to talk to Coach Dean?"

I slid out of the way, relieved that Ethan was taking control.

Chase rested his hand on the small of my back, and I flinched slightly.

Maiken tried to get around his brother, but Ethan blocked him. "Don't ruin your chance to play."

"You're not playing ball." Chase's rabid tone made me quiver.

Maiken's nostrils flared. "You're not the coach." Then his eyes softened, sucking me into a sea of blue. "Quinn, I'll see you later." Maiken and Ethan disappeared in the crowd.

Chase combed thick fingers through his floppy brown hair, shook off his ire, then held out his elbow. "Come on, gorgeous."

Shock rumbled through me like a bolt of lightning. I seriously had to look behind me to make sure he wasn't talking to someone else. I thought after I'd declined his invitation, he wouldn't want anything to do with me.

"You look confused," Chase said. "Let me make it clear again. I like you, Quinn. I told you last night I wouldn't give up. Besides, you said we could be friends. Are you taking that back?"

I stared at him as if he had ten heads. "No. I want to be friends."

He held out his elbow. "Good. Then let me escort you to a table."

I giggled as I became lightheaded. If people were gawking, I couldn't tell. I was afraid to look at anyone or turn around to see if Maiken was watching.

Chase stopped at the first empty table, which wasn't far from the one where Celia and I usually sat. The surrounding area had thinned out.

He pulled out my chair. "Would you reconsider going to my party as my friend?"

Unhooking my backpack, I sat down. If I did go as a *friend,* I would feel as though I were hurting Maiken, even though we weren't dating. Plus, I remembered what Celia had said: *I don't think boys know how to be friends, or at least I don't get that vibe from Chase.* I was new to all this attention from boys, and the more I studied Chase, the more I got the same vibe. He would want more from me than just friendship.

"I'm sorry. The answer is s-still n-no."

Sliding into the chair across from me, he frowned.

My heart pinched with the dull pain of sorrow. This boyfriend thing or friends-with-boys thing was weird and odd. The first boy had finally asked me out, and my answer was a big, fat no.

Time for a subject change.

"Why doesn't Tessa know that you invited me?"

He grinned, but it seemed fake. "I love my sister, but she can be a bitch. I didn't want her to give you any trouble."

"But if I showed up at your party, she would go—"

"Batshit crazy." That time, his grin seemed real. "Is that why you don't want to go?"

I shook my head, but maybe that was another reason I'd said no.

The bell rang. That was Chase's bell to head back to class since he was a junior. I still had twenty minutes before I had to be in chemistry.

Combing his fingers through his hair, he stood. "If you change your mind, you know where I live." Again, his gaze slid over me, giving me the impression he wanted to say or do something.

My cheeks heated until I glanced past Chase. I hopped up like a jumping jack. Chase followed my line of sight and straightened. Carter marched toward us with the scowl of the century. Fire flickered in his brown eyes, which were turning coppery.

I held up my hand as if I could stop my brother from attacking Chase. "Don't make a scene. I have two plus years in this school before I graduate, and I would like to get by without anyone remembering how much of a bully my brother can be." I never stuttered when it came to my brothers.

Carter looked down his long patrician nose, and his expression sent shivers down my spine. I was standing in front of a young version of my dad, and for that, I shivered again.

Chase intervened. "Carter, we've known each other a long time. You know I wouldn't do anything to hurt Quinn."

Carter quickly and sharply jerked his head then glowered at Chase. "You're right. I do. Because if you have any idea of making a spectacle of my sister or touching her without her consent, I will bury you. You would never make it to the NBA, let alone play college ball."

I wasn't sure how Carter could or would pull that off, but my brother didn't make idle threats.

Chase didn't react. There wasn't even an ounce of fear in his expression. I didn't know what to make of that. Maiken had run when Carter scared him off.

Carter addressed me. "I came over to tell you I'll be taking you home. We need all the help we can get with the trees until Liam and Maiken get done with basketball practice. Meet me at my truck after school." Then he swaggered off.

I wanted to cringe. All that needed to happen to make the day complete was for Tessa to show up and give us her two cents. At first, I thought the person Chase was eyeing behind Carter was Tessa until Celia called my name.

"See you later." Chase scurried off and disappeared in the throng of students leaving the cafeteria.

I puffed out my cheeks. Maybe I shouldn't date. My life was so much less dizzying without boys.

Celia stabbed a thumb over her shoulder. "What's going on?"

I plopped back into my seat. "Boys. I don't think I want to date."

Giggling, Celia commandeered Chase's chair. "So, dish, woman. How did Chase take your answer? Have you seen Maiken today?"

I filled her in on all the juicy details from the night before and that morning with Tessa, Maiken, and Chase.

She pushed her dark-framed glasses up on her nose. "You go from not having any boys notice you to two now." She let out a dreamy sigh. "Chase is handsome, but Maiken beats him."

I had to agree. But it wasn't only Maiken's sandy-blond hair and blue eyes that made him dreamy. His quiet demeanor was intriguing and drew me to him. I was beginning to understand why my brothers didn't like pushy girls. Granted, it wasn't as if I had a group of boys asking me out, but I wasn't sure yet how I felt about Chase not giving up on us as boyfriend and girlfriend.

Celia sat back. A streak of blond hair stood out among her dark strands, a trait she'd inherited from her dad, who had white-blond hair. "If you want to go to the party, my mom could use the help. That way, we both get to bask in the richness of the Stevenses' holiday gala."

I would rather go as a guest, but maybe working the party would be less nerve-racking and keep Tessa's evil eye off of me.

Chapter 16

Maiken

The Christmas tree business was slow that night. Mr. Thompson had said that weekends were the busiest, which meant I could make some cash. I had plans for spending a small amount on presents for my sisters and brothers and a special gift for Mom. Then I would put away the rest for school lunches and gas for the family car.

Mr. Thompson seemed in a cheerier mood than he had the night before when he'd chewed part of my butt off. I was relieved he hadn't reminded me not to get into trouble. I didn't plan on any trouble unless Chase showed up again. Part of me believed Chase would come by again just to get in my face and tell me that I wasn't going to play shooting guard unless it was over his dead body. I would like to think I wouldn't engage with him, but Chase Stevens was making me become someone I didn't recognize.

Despite my self-analysis, I replayed that afternoon on the basketball court over and over like a broken record.

Chase had stomped his foot as he'd shouted at Coach in front of the entire basketball team. "I'm the shooting guard. I'm the best one you've had in two years. He is *not* taking my position."

Coach had been stoked when I'd shown up in his office after school, ready to practice and take on my rightful position on the court.

"I'm the coach of this team. Maiken Maxwell will be the shooting guard. Once you see him in action, you'll agree."

"Never." Chase had spat venom as he'd stomped off and out of the gym.

The team had held their breath while Chase had thrown a tantrum. I'd been indifferent. I'd never seen Chase play, so I couldn't judge, nor could I brag that I was the better player. Coach, however, could. He'd seen my tapes. He'd seen Chase play. So he was the expert.

Regardless, I couldn't blame Chase for standing up for himself. If the tables had been turned, I would argue too. Actually, I'd done something similar in the seventh grade when the gym teacher had wanted to move me from center to shooting guard. In the end, he'd done it for my own benefit.

"You're a shooting guard, Maiken," he'd said. "You don't miss many shots, and you make every three-pointer."

The only reason I hadn't wanted to give up being a center for the school's basketball team was ego. I'd felt like a failure. Yet once I had changed positions, I understood what the gym teacher had seen in me. Maybe Chase would come to that same conclusion about himself.

Even Liam had said amid Chase's outburst that he would be an awesome point guard. "He knows the game and is an okay shooter, but he's a master of seeing the big picture on the court."

I'd asked why he hadn't played point guard before.

"Because of Alex," Liam had added. "Alex was the best."

Despite all that, one tiny problem remained. That animosity that Coach didn't want on the court was thicker than ever. I wasn't sure if I would last long on the team if Coach adhered to his ultimatum.

I knew Chase wasn't going to give up. I also knew I wouldn't let him walk all over me. The other problem between us was Quinn. I wouldn't say Quinn was a problem, but Chase and I were jockeying for the same girl. Well, he had made his intentions known, and I hadn't.

I had to choose my battles. Basketball had always been my first love. Girls had never been front and center in my life. Yet I was struggling with what was important to me—a girl or basketball.

The problem was I couldn't get Quinn out of my head. At lunch, I'd itched to sweep Quinn out of the room and away from Chase. My brother Ethan found it funny that I was crushing on a girl. "I've never seen you so into a chick before," he'd said as we left the cafeteria. "I like it."

I wasn't sure I did. She was making me crazy. I wanted to play with her long butterscotch hair. I wanted to feel her hand in mine again, and above all else, I was dying to kiss her.

None of that would happen if her brothers had a say in the matter. I couldn't blame Carter for protecting his sister. I would do the same with any boy who looked at my sisters the wrong way, although I wasn't too worried about Emma since she could probably deck a guy in two seconds flat. She had learned how to defend herself from Dad and from sparring with our fourteen-year-old brother, Marcus.

I needed to stop thinking about Quinn and focus on what I knew best, and that was basketball. Girls were too confusing anyway.

"I can help with other things around the farm if you have a need," I said to Mr. Thompson before I left.

He gave me one of his infamous mean expressions. "If you don't mind, can you take the box of apples down to the barn?" He stabbed a finger at the box on top of the counter inside the hut.

"Sure." I imagined the apples were for the horses. "Is Quinn down at the barn?"

He cocked one of his bushy eyebrows. "Do you like my daughter, son?"

I shrugged, but I knew full well I did. But I was afraid if I told him the truth, he might lay into me like Carter had, and I was more afraid of the elder Thompson than the younger one. For all I knew, Mr. Thompson would fire me if I said yes.

His Adam's apple bobbed. "It's a simple yes or no. I'm not going to fire you if that's why you won't answer."

"She's pretty."

He grinned as though in agreement. Then he lost his smile as he scrutinized me.

I shrank as nerves poked holes in my stomach. Even though he'd said he wouldn't fire me, I didn't believe him. I grabbed the box of apples. I could at least do that one final task before he let me go.

The more he studied me, the more I got a weird feeling. Or maybe he was trying to decide if I was good enough for his daughter.

"I'll take the box down to the barn." I got one foot out of the hut when he cleared his throat.

"Wait, son. I appreciate your honesty. After that interaction between you and the Stevens boy, it's hard not to see that both of you are smitten with Quinn. But I'll tell you like I told him. If you so much as hurt my daughter, I will take matters into my own hands."

Chase doesn't like your daughter. He's up to something. "You have nothing to worry about on my end. I would never hurt her. Anyway, Quinn likes Chase, not me." Oh, man. I sounded like a love-struck teenager.

You are!

He scratched the scruff on his face. "I tell my boys and Quinn to fight for what they want. You should do the same."

My mouth opened slightly. "Are you saying I should fight for Quinn?" *And what about Carter, your son, the boy who wants to tear off my head?*

"What I'm saying is don't let anyone get in the way of what you want."

Tires crunched on the gravel, causing my attention to dart to the parking lot.

My gaze lingered on the truck, relieved that the driver wasn't Chase. But I did a double take when Coach Dean got out.

"Go," Mr. Thompson said. "I got this."

Coach Dean's presence reminded me of something. "Sir, it's important to me that you know Chase lied to you yesterday. I'm not trying to take his position on the court." He'd already assumed I was trouble because of my name. I couldn't have him believing that I was a liar too.

"I know, son," Mr. Thompson said. "Sports is competitive, and I understand that as a new boy on the team, others can be threatened."

Whew came to mind as Coach Dean adjusted his ball cap then exchanged a handshake with Mr. Thompson.

"What brings you by, Coach?" Mr. Thompson asked. "Our poker night is Friday. Or did I miss something?"

Coach grinned. "I was hoping I could talk to Maiken here."

I was stuck on the idea of them playing poker and not the fact that he was there to see me. My dad had loved to play poker with his buddies.

Mr. Thompson patted Coach on the back. "Maiken's not on the clock. I need to finish up receipts."

"Let's take a walk," Coach said.

"I need to deliver this box to the barn," I said.

Coach waved his hand toward the snowy rolling hills. "Lead the way."

As we headed down to the barn, I asked, "What's this about?"

"I want you to play point guard instead of shooting guard."

I almost dropped the box. "Why the change? What happened after practice?" My stomach hurt all of a sudden. Coach had all but begged me to play shooting guard. "It's because of Chase's temper tantrum. Isn't it?" The anger coursing through me was so bright, it probably made me glow.

"Son, explain to me the difference between point guard and shooting guard."

I angled my head at Coach. "Is this a trick question?"

"Humor me."

We reached the barn, and I could hear Quinn inside talking to Apple. "Point guard has great ball-handling skills." I set the box of apples down on a small table right outside the open barn door. "He can maneuver the team during a play and is capable of three-pointers." I pulled my knit hat down over my years. "The shooting guard is the best shooter on the team from short or long distances."

"Exactly," he said. "Point guard is the leader of the team. Chase is not a leader. His outburst today showed me that. No matter how much he can play point guard, he wouldn't be very effective if he can't lead the plays."

I couldn't believe Chase hadn't shown his true colors to Coach before that day. Still, he had a point, although... "But according to some of the guys on the team, Chase would be a better point guard. Even Liam said Chase knows the game and is a master at seeing the big picture on the court."

Coach chuckled. "I would agree that Chase knows the game. But right now, he isn't going to see any picture since he's adamant about not giving up his position as shooting guard. And right now, I need to bring the team together not tear them apart. I want to win games. Don't you?"

No matter what position Chase played, I had a feeling he wouldn't be a team player with me as the point guard. "So it's either point guard or no position at all?"

He scratched his chin. "I could move Phil to point guard, but he's better at being a small forward."

Out of the corner of my eye, I saw Quinn gliding in our direction. Even Coach latched onto her and smiled as she approached.

Her nose and cheeks were red. Her hair was tied up on top of her head the way my mom had worn her hair when it was long. But what made my body fire on all cylinders was her smile when we locked eyes.

"Hi," she said. "What's going on? Coach, what brings you out to the farm? It's not poker night."

With a teasing grin, he said, "Someone told me I could find Maiken here. Thank you."

She fixated on her muddy boots. "You're welcome."

"Do you want to help me convince Maiken that point guard will suit him?"

Kissing Quinn might suit me better. Maybe I had my priorities all wrong. Maybe I should put a girl first and basketball second. After all,

I wasn't sure I would be any good at point guard. Sure, I could handle the ball, lead the team, and shoot, but I loved playing shooting guard.

"I'm n-not sure I'm the r-right person to do that," Quinn said.

I had an ego like any other person, but mine wouldn't be derailed at all if Quinn threw in her two cents.

"Give it your best shot," Coach said.

All I could think about was that day she'd spewed facts about the Celtics. Come to think of it, I'd asked her if she liked basketball, and she'd never answered me.

She focused on Coach as she spoke to me. "Maybe playing both p-positions will get you noticed q-quicker by colleges."

I smirked at how cute she was when she was nervous.

"What Quinn is trying to say," Coach said, "is that combo players in the sport are in extremely high demand and popular."

"It's like a switch-hitter in baseball," Quinn added. "Teams like s-switch-hitters."

I was dizzy all of a sudden. Not from them teaming up on me, but Quinn's knowledge of not only basketball but baseball too.

Coach winked at her. "Exactly. I've got to run. Maiken, think about it." Then he strolled back up the path.

I was at a loss for words as Quinn and I stood outside the barn, watching Coach fade in the distance.

Chapter 17

Quinn

I dared not look at Maiken. I hated that Coach had put me on the spot. I wasn't the expert on all things basketball. Still, Maiken's gaze was cemented straight ahead, and I couldn't tell if he was shocked or disappointed by my advice. He probably thought I was siding with Chase when I was only speaking the truth about what I knew from hearing my brothers talk about the game.

The cold bit into my face as a snowflake landed on my nose. More freezing temperatures were predicted overnight, but I didn't recall snow being in the forecast. Maybe if we had another snow day, I could go ice-skating. I was sure the lake behind the Maxwell house was frozen solid or close to it.

"I h-have to put a blanket on Apple." I seriously had to find a way not to stutter around Maiken. Granted, I stuttered whenever I was nervous, but I was doing it more and more lately.

Maiken picked up the box of apples as he followed me in. The heat from one of the stand-up heaters radiated over me as we walked by.

I pointed at the table in between Apple's stall and Oscar's, her companion. "Can you set the box down there?" I disappeared into Apple's stall and covered her.

Maiken watched with a blank expression, which was a far cry from the fear he'd shown in the barn the other day when he had been scared out of his mind. "Did you feed the horses already?"

"Carter did earlier. So are you going to play point guard?" I was dying to know what he thought about my input on the matter.

He leaned on the rail of the stall, comfortable and casual. "Do you think I should?"

I walked out of the stall. "It's your decision."

He straightened, his blue gaze searing me. "Or do you want Chase to play shooting guard?"

My stomach knotted. "W-Why." I took a breath. "Never mind." I didn't know how to handle a jealous boy. I didn't want to be snarky. Instead, I took his hand, a habit that was slowly forming when I was around him, which didn't make any sense. I was nervous to speak around him but brave enough to take his hand. Boy, that was a contradiction. Yet I didn't let go no matter how much my stomach churned. "Come on."

Maiken's calloused fingers swallowed my small hand. "I should go." His protest was weak at best.

I tugged on his arm. "I want to show you something."

He searched the barn, no doubt for Carter.

"Carter isn't here," I felt compelled to say. If Carter so much as showed up and started trouble, I would do something drastic like tattle on him to Momma. She could always get Carter to listen to reason. If she couldn't, I had no hope of dating that year. The good news was that Carter was a senior, so he wouldn't be around to scare off boys my junior or senior year.

His tight features loosened. "I have homework."

I did too, but I would drop everything to hang out with Maiken. He let go of my hand, and I mentally pouted. I started for the loft, hoping he would follow. I was relieved when I heard his footsteps behind me. When we reached the stairs, which were at the opposite end of the barn, he coughed. I was used to the smell of horses, manure, and hay floating in the air, but he obviously wasn't.

I climbed the stairs and switched on the light at the top of the landing. "Over here." I padded across the wood planks to the open door that overlooked the hills of our property. Snowflakes floated to the ground as a biting wind blew in, stirring up the remnants of hay that were strewn over the floor.

I moved the telescope, a gift Momma and Daddy had given me for Christmas last year, and pointed the lens toward the sky.

Maiken looked around. "What did you want to show me?"

I peeked through the lens, even though clouds covered the stars. I sighed heavily. "Maybe another time. The stars aren't out."

He stood close to the edge, glancing out. "Great view."

The view was even prettier at sunset, especially in the summertime when streaks of oranges, purples, and blues painted the horizon at dusk.

He sniffed the brisk outside air, seeming content, relaxed, and looking so dreamy with the way his hair poked out from his knit hat. "It's quiet up here."

The loft was my hideaway, a place I could come when I wanted to think or read or even do homework after tending to my chores.

"So how do you know so much about basketball?" he asked evenly. His attention was anywhere but on me.

"Um, brothers, Dad, uncles, and cousins are all into the game. Sports is big in my family."

He seemed to freeze at the word family.

I joined him, admiring the land I'd known my whole life and catching a glimpse of Maiken out of the corner of my eye. He looked sad. I wanted to hug him and tell him everything would be okay, but I didn't know that for sure. I hadn't lost Daddy, and I would die if I did. Nevertheless, my heart flew against my ribs. *Bang! Bang! Bang!* In the silence of the loft, I was sure he could hear it too.

"I'm sorry about your dad," I finally said.

He sighed. "Thank you." His tone was somber. "I miss him."

The need to hug him grew stronger. "Do you want to talk about it?" Sometimes people felt better if they had a friend who would listen to them.

He grinned through his despair. "Your black eyes are healing nicely."

The color was now a yucky yellow, but makeup had saved me from all the whispers and stares in school.

I picked up a piece of hay. "Did you know that the word family came into the English language in the fifteenth century?"

His warm fingers landed on my chin. "Quinn." He said my name in a husky tone, and my legs began to shake. I'd never fainted before, but my head felt dizzy. "You're pretty."

I stopped breathing, or maybe I was breathing too heavy, or maybe he had me under a spell. When Chase had told me I was pretty, I'd felt special. But Maiken saying the same thing made me feel different, excited. A current of warmth exploded in my belly.

Maiken pressed his lips into a thin line. "Are you going to be Chase's girl?"

That warmth turned to ice.

I don't want to be Chase's girlfriend. I want to be yours.

Footsteps clobbered up the steps. "Quinn," Carter called. "Are you up here?"

I cursed in my head. I never swore. But Carter must have had his Maiken radar on.

Maiken jumped away from me as if I had some sort of disease.

"I'm s-sorry about how Carter treated you the other night," I said in a whisper.

Carter appraised us as if he were my dad. "What's going on here?"

I snarled. "We're talking."

Carter wagged a gloved finger between us, narrowing his coppery eyes. "Looks to me like you two are getting pretty close."

Maiken rubbed his hands down his legs. "I should go. It's getting late."

"Damn right it's getting late." Carter's tone was hateful.

"I'll walk you out," I said to Maiken while baring my teeth at my brother.

Maiken's long legs ate up the distance to the top of the steps before he barreled down them as if he were being chased by a madman.

I couldn't help but let out a soft laugh. That madman was none other than Carter. I gripped my hips. "You're a jerk, Carter." Then I sprinted out, hoping to catch Maiken before he left.

"You shouldn't chase boys," Carter yelled. "It's not ladylike."

It was all I could do to refrain from giving my brother the finger.

Maiken had gotten all the way to the parking lot of the farm store by the time I caught up with him.

"Carter is just being a big brother."

Maiken grabbed the handle of the driver's door. "I'll see you at school tomorrow." Then in a flash, he was driving away.

I stomped back to the barn with the intention of giving Carter a piece of my mind when Bo came barreling up to me. "Where did you come from?" I scratched his ears. "You should be in the house." I lifted my gaze to find Momma standing on the front porch.

"I let him out," she said. "Everything okay between you and Maiken?"

I jogged to the house, and Bo ran with me. "Carter keeps scaring him off." I wasn't one to tattle, but extreme measures called for some sort of help.

She held out her arm. "Let's go inside. We can talk over a hot chocolate."

No amount of hot chocolate would stop Carter from being my big brother or Maiken from running every time Carter showed up.

Chapter 18

Maiken

Snow, snow, and more snow. The fluffy white stuff was piling up outside, and school had been canceled once again. The way we were going, we wouldn't finish school until July.

I threaded my hands through my hair as I walked into the kitchen. I stood for a moment and listened. The house was quiet. No kids were screaming, fighting, giggling, or even running around.

I yawned as I padded across the wood floor to the sliding glass door. The Suburban was in the driveway with snow piled up to the top of the tires. The spaces next to our car were clear, and tire tracks were stamped in the snow. Maybe Uncle Martin had taken the family somewhere. But if that were the case, Mom would've left me a note, or someone would've woken me up to tell me.

I started to get something to drink when I spied Mom trudging through the snow alongside the garage. She beamed up at me. Her face was rosy, and her pants and boots were covered in snow. It looked as though she had been in a snowball fight.

I opened the door for her. A frigid wind blew in, causing me to bite my lip.

She stomped her boots on the carpet before removing her winter gear. "You finally got out of bed. It's almost lunchtime."

After Mom had informed me I didn't have school that morning, I'd gone back to sleep.

I rubbed my bare arms as I went over to the fridge. "Where is everyone?"

She blew into her hands before she filled the teapot with water. "Your aunt and uncle took Charlotte, Harlan, and Maple to the Thompson farm to ride horses. Marcus and Jasper are out exploring the property, Ethan is helping Kade clean out the boathouse, and Emma is watching Quinn skate. She's such a good skater too."

My body instantly warmed at the mention of Quinn's name. "Quinn?" Then I thought about how I'd run like the wind from Carter. I was embarrassed to even face her. Part of me was a little intimidated by him, but the other part of me didn't want to lose my job. It sucked knowing that I could lose my job at any moment if I did something stupid like kiss Quinn. When Carter had shown up in the loft, my lips had been so close to Quinn's.

Mr. Thompson told you to go after what you want when you were discussing how you liked Quinn. So in a way, you have his approval. Tell that to Carter. I didn't think he would agree with his dad.

My mom's brown eyes had several questions swimming in them. "You like her." It was more of a statement than a question. "You've never had any interest in girls before." She turned on the gas burner. The *tick, tick, tick* sound filled the room before the burner ignited.

I shrugged, even though I knew full well I liked Quinn. It was odd to discuss girls with my mom, only because I hadn't dated a girl yet, and talk of girls or the birds and the bees had been reserved for my dad.

Mom's cold hand on my face brought me back to the present. "Talk to me. Tell me about Quinn."

I poured some orange juice in a glass. "There's nothing to tell." *You're lying again. Tell her how you love when Quinn stutters and how cute she is when she gets nervous. Tell your mom how something is happening inside you whenever you're around Quinn or how if you don't kiss Quinn soon, you might explode—not in the erection kind of way, but in the "I might die" kind of way.*

I knew I was being dramatic, but the feelings were new, odd, and exciting. I had hardly been hungry since I'd met her. I couldn't stop thinking about the two of us, and I'd lain in bed last night wondering how her lips would feel against mine. Sadly, though, I didn't know how to kiss, and I didn't know if Quinn would run if I dared try. I'd listened to my friends back in North Carolina and to Ethan talk about kissing girls—how they taste, how off the charts it was when your tongue touched a girl's, how a girl's body felt soft, her hair silky. One friend had even explained a girl's scent.

Quinn smelled like cherry blossoms. I knew her skin was soft since I'd touched her chin the night before. I loved how her amber eyes were golden when the light hit her in the right way, and what really got me all tensed up in a good way was when she spat out facts, especially about sports.

Mom snapped her fingers. "Maiken, where did you go?"

I needed to shake off Quinn before my jeans got too tight, so I chugged the orange juice. "You said Ethan is helping Kade clean out the boathouse?"

Mom had a tea bag in her hand. "You should go down and help. It's going to be a game room for everyone."

And hopefully a place where I could go to be alone or maybe invite Quinn to join me.

I set my glass in the sink. "I'll go get my coat."

The teapot began whistling.

"Maiken, before you go, I've been meaning to ask you. Are you going to play basketball?"

I hiked a shoulder. "Coach wants me to play point guard."

She poured hot water into her mug. "But you're a shooting guard."

If my dad were there, he would say the same thing.

I sat down on a barstool. "Can we move back to North Carolina?" Until that moment, I hadn't thought about moving back. The idea of returning to my old school and playing for my old team sounded wonderful, though. *If you do, then you won't get to see Quinn.* I didn't know how I felt about that.

S.B. ALEXANDER

My mom brought her tea over to the island, angling her head. "You don't like it here?"

When we'd first arrived, I'd been all for being the big brother and helping my family, who I'd thought would be moping around a lot. I was wrong. They all seemed to be adapting to their new surroundings just fine. Even my brother Ethan wasn't brooding so much anymore over Dad or his recent breakup.

"Do you?" I asked. To me, it was more important for Mom to be happy than me.

"Maiken, my life is you and your brothers and sisters. If they're happy, then I'm happy, and right now, your brothers and sisters really like it here. But I'll be honest with you. I wouldn't mind moving to Georgia to be near Aunt Denise. The cold and snow don't exactly thrill me either." She took a sip of her tea. "What's bothering you, though?" Mom always noticed the tiniest mood swings.

All of a sudden, tears filled my eyes. "I miss Dad."

She skirted the edge of the island and sat on the stool next to me. "And you think moving to the South will take away your pain?"

I swallowed hard. "I don't know."

Her cold hand covered mine. "Maiken."

The softness in her voice, and the tears in her eyes were all I needed to let out all the heartache that had been building. I had mourned when I was alone, but I hadn't full-on bawled in front of Mom.

She threw her arms around me. "You can't hold things in, not something this big." She sniffled. "You need to talk about how you're feeling."

I buried my face in her chest and sobbed.

She rubbed my back. "It's okay to cry and let go. I'm here for you. We all are."

But I wanted my dad. I wanted to see him sitting in the bleachers at one of my basketball games. I wanted to talk to him about girls. I wanted to hear him laugh when Harlan, Jr. came running into the room with a frog in his hand. I wanted to see him and Mom together again.

I eased away. "Are we moving to Georgia?"

She wiped tears from my cheeks. "We need our own place. Your dad's life insurance should be coming through soon. But I'm undecided on whether we find a house around here or near your aunt Denise. What do you think?"

"I liked living in North Carolina. We had a nice life there."

She dragged a finger through her dark-blond hair, which was rather curly that morning, then resumed her spot on the stool. "We were happy in North Carolina, but that was with your dad." She blinked away a tear. "I told you that we took your uncle Martin up on his offer so we could get on our feet. But the real reason is you boys need some structure as you grow into men. Uncle Martin and maybe his sons can help, especially you as the oldest. I'm not saying they're your father's replacement, but your uncle has four sons that have turned into good men."

I liked Kade. When he'd first come into my bedroom to chat, I thought he would try to fill my dad's shoes. Hell, I'd thought Uncle Martin would too. But both of them had given me space.

It was my turn to hold my mom's hand. "Wherever you decide to buy a house, I won't give you any trouble. I want to be the man in the family."

She smiled, but it never reached her eyes. "You're a good boy, Maiken. But I want you to play basketball. Your dad would've wanted that too. Financially, we're okay for now, although I will have to find a job later down the line."

Before my mom and dad had gotten married, Mom had studied law. But she and Dad had made the decision that she would be a full-time mom when Dad had enlisted in the military.

She sipped her tea. "I have some calls to make."

I kissed her on the cheek. "I love you."

She grabbed my arm as I was about to walk away. "Do me a favor. Play basketball."

I gave her a weak smile. It wasn't that I didn't want to play. I just wasn't sure if I would be any good as a point guard. More than that,

Chase would brag and taunt me about how he'd gotten his way in keeping his position as shooting guard. Then I would throw the first punch. If that happened, I wouldn't shoot another basketball my entire high school career, which meant no college ball.

Maybe it was time to put my ego and emotions aside and do the one thing that my dad had wanted me to—play basketball.

Chapter 19

Quinn

My nose was running like the faucet Liam always left running, something Momma got mad over. His excuse had always been that he was waiting for the water to warm up.

"Not for five minutes," Mom had scolded.

It wasn't that we were rationing water since we had a well on our property, but the possibility existed that our well could run dry, at least according to Daddy.

I wiped my nose with the back of my gloved hand. The temps were below zero that day, and aside from my face feeling like a block of ice, my body was rather warm from spinning and gliding around the lake on my skates. I hadn't tried any of my jumps or even my routine that I had done a time or two when I'd been competing. Today was just for fun, but I did miss skating. I enjoyed the wind at my face, Beethoven or Mozart in my ears, and the sense that I was flying on ice.

Maybe Momma was right, and I could skate and make valedictorian.

Emma Maxwell waved from the shore behind the Maxwell estate. I waved back as I skated over to her. She'd been watching me for the last thirty minutes. If I were being honest, I'd been eyeing the boathouse and the entire property to see if Maiken would show up. I'd seen Kade and Ethan go in and out, but no Maiken.

Maybe he'd gone over to my farm. Before I'd left, Momma had told me that some of the Maxwell kids were stopping by with Eleanor and Martin to pet the horses. Then again, Maiken wasn't exactly enamored with horses, and his shift at the Christmas tree stand didn't start until later that afternoon. I also knew he didn't have basketball practice. Liam had mentioned at breakfast that Coach had canceled practice until Monday.

I wiped my nose again as I slowed to a stop on the edge of the shore, pulling out my earbuds. "Hey."

Emma was wrapped in several layers, including a bright-yellow knitted hat that highlighted her brown hair. She didn't look much like Maiken. I suspected she'd taken after her dad since her mom had blondish hair that was a cross between Emma's color and Maiken's sandy blond.

Her glossy lips glistened beneath the noon sun. "Wow! You know how to skate. Did you ever compete?"

"I did up until the eighth grade."

"Why don't you now? You're really good."

So was Tessa. "I want to be a doctor, so school comes first. And colleges don't offer skating scholarships." At least the schools I wanted to attend didn't. Still, she didn't need to know that skating cost a ton of money that my parents didn't have.

"You know, Maiken wants to go into the NBA, but he might not get into college because of his grades."

I tilted my head. "Is he failing?" If he was, he couldn't play sports. The school had a strict policy on grades. Anyone playing a sport had to have a C or higher.

"I don't really know," Emma said.

The thought of tutoring him flittered through my mind but then vanished. I would stutter the entire time if I tutored Maiken.

"Can you teach me how to skate?" she asked.

I was the last person to teach anyone how to skate. Besides, skating was a sport that people had to learn by doing, at least the basics of not falling down.

"We have an ice rink in town where you can give it a try. I'm not the best teacher, but we can go this weekend if you'd like." Aside from homework and chores, I didn't have much else planned. "Celia will probably join us if that's okay." Celia loved to boy watch, and the rink was usually packed on Saturday nights.

She clapped. "I would love that. Maybe I could get Maiken to come." She waggled her eyebrows.

I wobbled on my skates, more so when I spotted Maiken swaggering down from the house. My heart pinwheeled, and my mouth became dry.

Emma followed my line of sight. "Speak of the devil."

Maiken's hair curled around the edges of his navy-blue knit hat. I sighed at how handsome he was.

"He likes you," Emma said. "He's never had a girlfriend or liked a girl before you."

I flinched her way, and when I did, my feet came out from under me. Luckily, with my three layers of clothing, I hardly felt the hard surface on my bottom. But I sure felt the heat pinch my cheeks as embarrassment settled in. I dared not look at Maiken, afraid he would be laughing at me.

"Oh my," Emma cooed, holding out her hand. "Here, I'll help you."

"I got this." It was best I pushed myself up on two blades. Otherwise, I would only take her down with me. Besides, I'd had plenty of practice falling and getting up from all the years on skates. I dug the toe of my skate into the ice and pushed upright, quick and fast, before peeking to see where Maiken was or if he was laughing.

He stood holding on to the rail of the steps leading up to the boathouse, watching me.

I wanted to look away. I wanted to feel the wind on my face to cool the heat that was building to an inferno from equal parts shyness and embarrassment.

Emma waved her arm as if she were summoning an ambulance. "Maiken, get over here."

I skated in a small circle for nothing more than to shake off my nerves.

Maiken strutted over. He was wearing jeans and army boots, and his open coat displayed the word "Starlight" on his T-shirt. I wondered what Starlight meant. Maybe it was a band I hadn't heard of. I did listen to classical music when I skated, but my taste in music as a whole was geared more toward seventies and eighties rock and roll, thanks in part to my granny, who loved that era and genre of music. Often times, Celia laughed at Granny when she had the Eagles playing when we visited.

I came to a stop at the edge of the lake where the ice met the snow-covered ground.

Maiken sidled up to Emma with a fraught expression. Maybe he didn't want anything to do with me after Carter had all but chased him out of the loft. Now my own ire was bubbling to the surface. Momma had told me during our conversation last night that I should talk to Carter and somehow make him understand that he couldn't keep boys away from me forever.

But thoughts of talking to Carter vanished when I locked eyes with Maiken. He looked as though he'd been crying. Sadness supplanted my anger.

"What's wrong?" Emma asked. "Did something happen?" Her bubbly attitude flew away with the hard wind that whipped around us.

Maiken reared back. "Nothing happened."

She leaned into her brother and whispered something in his ear.

"I'm fine," he said.

I didn't believe him, but it wasn't any of my business to ask questions.

"Quinn is taking me skating this weekend," Emma said. "Do you want to go?"

Please say yes. Images of Maiken and me holding hands as we skated around the rink danced in my head.

He swung his gaze from me to Emma. "I can't. I have to work until closing this weekend."

Maybe it was for the best. If I knew Tessa, she would be at the rink, showing off like she usually did. Suddenly, I was regretting my invitation to take Emma. Tessa would only taunt me or brag about how Maiken was going to her party as her date. I still wasn't sure if he'd accepted her invitation despite the fact that he didn't do parties.

"Well, you're not working the night of the Stevenses' party," Emma said. "We're going, right?"

My legs almost gave out again. He *was* going with Tessa.

"Maiken," Ethan said from the deck of the boathouse. "We need your help moving the foosball table."

Maiken pinned me with a look as though he were trying to decipher my thoughts. I'd never gotten the chance to answer his question about being Chase's girl or tell him I wasn't going to the party with Chase. Now it really didn't matter if he knew or not. He probably didn't care.

Sticking out my chin, I held back some tears that were itching to spill and skated off. At that moment, I was glad I had my skates on. It was a fast getaway, and no one could chase me.

"Quinn," Emma shouted.

I spun around then skated backward as I watched Maiken saunter up to his brother. I wondered if liking a boy was supposed to be so difficult or if getting my feelings sandblasted was part of liking a boy. I'd always thought it was supposed to be exciting and thrilling and that I would feel like dying if the boy I liked didn't kiss me.

I was dying. I'd never been kissed before, but I wanted my first time to be with Maiken. I wanted to be his girl.

I shoved my earbuds in and let Beethoven calm me as I concentrated on nothing but trying not to cry. I failed as one tear fell then two.

After several laps around the lake, I decided to head home. Emma had left, the backyard was empty, and if Maiken and his brother were in the boathouse, I couldn't tell. I changed into my boots, packed my skates into my bag, and started to leave when Maiken came out of the boathouse.

"Do you need a ride home?" His blue eyes were crystal clear, not cloudy like before.

"I was going to call Liam to pick me up." My brother had dropped me off that morning.

"If you want to hang out until I have to be at the farm, we can get some hot chocolate and play some foosball, or there's a pinball machine in the funhouse."

A flush spread across my cheeks. "Is that what the b-boathouse is called?"

"Kade tells me that his wife dubbed it the funhouse when they were in high school."

I didn't have to be home right away. It was Friday, and there was no school, and homework could wait until the weekend. The funhouse sounded wonderful, mainly because Carter wouldn't show up unexpectedly and scare off Maiken.

"Sure."

He grinned like a boy who had just won the state basketball championship game of the year, and because of that, I tingled all over.

Chapter 20

Maiken

I swallowed some nerves as Quinn and I entered the funhouse. I was about to spend time with the one girl who had my insides in a pile of mush.

Kade lounged on the couch, which was positioned underneath the window, and Ethan was parked on top of the edge of the foosball table. I wished I could say I'd put in my two cents helping Kade and Ethan clean the place, but my only contribution had been helping them move the foosball machine from one side of the room to the other.

Regardless, when I'd walked into the funhouse, I'd been blown away at how cool and cozy the space was, especially the view of the lake, on which I'd focused special attention while watching Quinn skate. My mom had been right. Quinn was good. I'd been in awe at how graceful she was and how she seemed to be in her element as if no one or nothing around her existed. I knew that feeling on the basketball court when I tuned out the crowd.

Kade pushed to his feet and set his light-brown gaze on Quinn. "I saw you out there. Are you taking up skating again?"

"Do you compete?" I asked the most beautiful girl I'd ever laid eyes on.

She dropped her gaze to the tiled floor. "Not anymore."

Bummer. I wouldn't mind watching her skate forever.

Ethan swung his legs back and forth, much like our brother Harlan always did when Mom set him on the kitchen counter so he could watch her make dinner. "I hear Tessa Stevens skates."

Quinn visibly tensed. "She's good." Despite her stiff posture, Quinn sounded envious.

Kade smoothed a hand over his honey-colored hair. "She might be, but I would bet you could give her a run for her money."

Quinn's eyes became as big as basketballs. "I doubt that."

"You shouldn't shortchange yourself," Kade said.

I had a feeling Quinn and Tessa had butted heads because of skating. Maybe that was one of the reasons why Quinn didn't compete anymore or why they'd become enemies.

Ethan hopped off the table. "Yeah, you should show Tessa that you're just as good or better. Right, Maiken?"

I couldn't disagree if skating was what Quinn wanted to do. Mom and Dad were the kind of parents that had never pushed us into anything. We'd had some friends whose parents insisted that their kid play baseball or football or whatever.

"Kids fail when parents pressure them," Dad had said.

My hand found its way to Quinn's. "I think we need to back off and let Quinn decide for herself."

Quinn grasped my hand as if to say thank you.

Kade gave me a proud look as he puffed out his chest. I was really beginning to feel as if Kade were my dad. "Maiken's right. Ethan, I need your help in the garage."

Ethan regarded Quinn then me with a grin the size of Texas. I knew what my brother was thinking. If we could mind-speak, he would say, "way to go, bro" and "it's about time."

Once Ethan and Kade were gone, Quinn let go of my hand as if I were burning her. Hell, she sure was making me extremely warm.

Her head swiveled like one of those bobbleheads that my grandfather had in the back of his car. "This place is a-amazing."

I thought so too. Aside from the foosball table that was the center of attention, a pinball machine was positioned in between the half-bath and the kitchen. A round card table was tucked in the corner adjacent to the door, and a couch and two recliners decorated the space. I couldn't wait to hang out there with my siblings and maybe Quinn too.

Sniffling, she sashayed over to the leather couch.

"Do you need a tissue? I'm sure there's one in the bathroom."

She pulled off her gloves. "I'm fine. D-did you know that when you inhale cold, dry air, the moist tissue inside your nose increases the fluid p-production?"

I chuckled. "Is there anything you don't know?" I took off my coat and joined her, but I sat on the opposite end of the couch. I was afraid I might kiss her if I got too close.

She sat prim and proper—hands in her lap, spine straight, holding her bottom lip hostage with her teeth. "Sure. I don't know a lot a-about you."

There wasn't much to know about me. "What do you want to know?" I would tell her anything. I had no secrets.

When she removed her hat, her cherry scent wafted in the air, and as if that was the trigger to pull me to her, I slid over and onto the cushion beside her.

She didn't move, but her body went rigid. "H-have you e-ever been on a d-date?"

Slowly, a grin formed as I studied her like she was a piece of art. My history teacher at my last school had a thing for old-world paintings, and she would bring in one or two from the era we'd been studying. She'd taught us to really look at the details, and I couldn't help but do the same with Quinn. She was a beautiful piece of art for sure— small nose, long lashes, heart-shaped lips, shiny hair, and... I dared not go lower than her face, although secretly I had when she hadn't been looking, and she definitely had rounded, nice-sized breasts.

She popped up, ready to run.

I latched onto her arm. "Where are you going?"

She hadn't run the night before when I'd been an inch from her. It'd been me who had run as if Apple were chasing me.

She gnawed her lip. "I-I should get home."

I pulled her to me. When I did, she lost her balance and fell on top of me. She scrambled to get up, but she wasn't going anywhere. Carter wasn't on the property, which meant he wouldn't walk through the door, although one of my siblings might. Still, they wouldn't scold Quinn or me.

"I've never been on a date before," I whispered in her ear, inhaling her essence.

As if I'd said the magic words, she melted into me and pressed her small hands against my chest. "Really?"

"You don't believe me?"

She angled her head and scrutinized me. "Is that why you ran out last night? Or are you afraid of Carter?"

Her nose was red, her eyes watered, and her lips were glossy—lips that I wanted to taste. I would bet the stuff she had on her lips tasted like cherries.

"A little bit of both. I respect your brother and how he doesn't want any guy to touch you. Rather than get into it with him, I just thought it would be better if I left. I'm sorry I ran, though. I should've handled the situation a bit better." *More like a man.* Her dad had told me to go after what I wanted when we'd been talking about Quinn. So in retrospect, I had his blessing, although he hadn't come out and said it.

Her tongue snaked out.

I swallowed hard as the need to finally kiss her overpowered every sense I had, but I didn't know how to kiss, which was partly why I'd left so abruptly the night before.

It can't be that hard. You press your lips to hers.

Ethan had bragged that kissing a girl for the first time was exciting and a little nail-biting since he didn't know what was going through the girl's mind. He said he was always preoccupied with whether he was doing it right and if she liked the kiss.

"Did you know that a full-on French kiss involves all th-thirty-four muscles in the f-face?"

I flopped my head back and laughed. She followed suit, giggling. As though that were the icebreaker, she leaned in and mashed her lips to mine.

I froze like the ice that was outside the window. But when she tried to push her tongue into my mouth, I opened freely. I saw stars, bright, big, and dreamy. I was floating on a cloud or maybe to another planet, one where it was only Quinn and me. I was lost in how her tongue was doing things that were new and exciting, and my groin was on board too.

I followed her lead and explored every crevice of her mouth. She whimpered, and I lost all control. My hands went in her hair. My fingers slipped through her long strands, which felt just how I'd imagined—soft and silky.

I had no idea what I was doing, but my body seemed to be guiding me. Hell, I had a full-on erection. I should've been embarrassed, but I wasn't. I didn't care. I wanted this girl in so many ways, but I knew I had to tamp down my libido and keep things to kissing. Besides, I couldn't even think about sex. We were too young. We hardly knew each other, and sex wasn't something to take lightly, at least according to my dad.

"Son, make sure your first time is special for both you and the girl. And do not force her into anything unless you two agree. And never have unprotected sex unless you're married."

I'd been thirteen at the time my dad had given me the birds-and-the-bees speech.

But speech aside, he'd never mentioned the physical feelings involved with kissing or otherwise. My head was spinning, and my heart was doing the same. Quinn was suddenly having her way with me.

Holy hell. I think I've been living under a rock. Ethan had the right idea when it came to girls.

She broke the kiss and dragged her lips up to my ear. "We should stop."

We should, especially because her brother Carter would throw a fit if he found out I'd kissed his baby sister.

I gripped her hips. "You're right. Let's get that hot chocolate." If we stayed in the funhouse or she stayed on top of me, I couldn't promise I would be a gentleman. I lifted her up as I stood. "I need to use the bathroom first." *And try to get my hard-on to go down.*

Her gaze traveled down to my crotch. "Oh."

I grinned, lacking any mortification I'd expected to feel from a girl knowing I'd gotten hard around her.

Quinn's cheeks glowed pink as she emitted a low laugh.

My grin got wider.

More awkwardness chipped away between us.

Nevertheless, I ducked into the bathroom, splashed some water on my face, and took in some deep breaths, willing my erection to subside. The bathroom didn't have a mirror, so I couldn't tell how I looked, but I sure did know how I felt. It was as if my eyes had been opened to a whole new world, and I wanted more of Quinn.

Five minutes later, I found Quinn on the couch, legs crossed underneath her as she texted on her phone.

I cleared my throat as I rested a hip on the foosball table.

Her gaze went straight to my belt then below. Her face reddened.

I smirked. She was so pretty with that shy look she seemed to wear most of the time around me.

"So are you going with Tessa to her party?" Quinn asked without an ounce of stuttering.

Maybe I'd kissed the nervous habit out of her.

I debated whether to sit next to her. If I did, then I would kiss her again. Then I would get another hard-on, and I was afraid I wouldn't be able to rein in my urges. "This party is getting out of control."

Her throat bobbed. "I'm not going to the party. I declined Chase's offer."

Fireworks went off in my head along with an image of me pumping my fist in the air. "I thought you liked him."

"As a friend."

"Does he know that?"

She nodded. "He's okay with it."

I doubted that. Chase had seemed serious when he'd told Quinn he liked her in front of Liam and me.

"So Tessa," she said, not looking at me. "Are you her date?"

I crossed the carpeted floor and dropped down beside her. "I'm not going to that party."

"You don't know Tessa. She doesn't take no for an answer."

I slid my hand over to hers. "Tessa doesn't control me." *You do, though.*

She arched her back slightly. My attention rounded to her breasts and how her sweater molded to them. Oh, man. I had to get it together. One kiss, and I was already thinking bad thoughts and looking where I shouldn't.

Quinn snapped her fingers. "Maiken?"

I blinked. "Sorry. I was thinking." *About you and me and kissing and so much more.*

She frowned. "D-did I make you mad?"

"Not at all." But really she was making me downright mad inside.

Chapter 21

Quinn

The music pumped out of the speakers, sounding hollow over the drone of voices in the skating rink.

I'd kissed a boy—a hot boy who'd kissed me back. That thought was on repeat in my head while the rest of the world around me was nonexistent. I touched my cheek as I skated on somewhat shaky legs. It felt as if my face were filled with hot lava as I thought of how I'd taken advantage of Maiken. Momma wouldn't have been proud, and neither would Granny. She would say I was a hussy.

Celia slapped me on the arm. "Hey, pay attention, or else you're going to fall."

Tessa would enjoy that immensely if she were at the rink. Then again, the place didn't close for another three hours. So she still could show up and be her usual witchy self and show off on the ice.

In between thinking about Maiken, I had spent time noodling over whether I wanted to give ice-skating a go again. Emma had been cheering me on, not only by the lake the day before but as soon as she'd gotten to the rink. She'd talked nonstop about the Olympics and how she loved watching the skaters and that I should consider getting serious about the sport.

Emma skated up to me. "Where are you going?" As soon as she'd put on skates and hit the ice, I could see she was a natural. She'd fallen once but had then taken off as if she'd been skating all her life.

Both Celia and Emma followed me to the exit.

"I need a break. You two skate." If I didn't sit down, my legs would give out at any second, and that second would be when Tessa decided to show up.

Emma smirked at me with her red nose shining beneath the rink's bright lights. It was as though she knew Maiken and I had kissed.

Oh my God. Maiken had told her. I hadn't even told Celia yet.

I narrowed my eyes at the pretty Maxwell girl. "What?"

"Maiken looked like you when he walked in the house yesterday."

The lava burning my cheeks had quadrupled.

Celia gaped. "Did you and Maiken do something? You did. Didn't you? I can see it on your face. I knew it. Why didn't you call me?" She all but ran off the ice, nearly falling into me as I dropped down on one of the benches that lined one side of the rink.

Emma stayed planted on the ice but watched me intently. Her brown eyes got bigger, and she practically salivated to hear what came out of my mouth next. She'd said Maiken had never had a girlfriend or liked a girl before me. I was relieved to hear him say he'd never been on a date before. That had made me feel a little less awkward. Okay, a lot less awkward since I'd made the first move.

Celia huffed beside me, crossing one leg over the other. "Well, chica? Dish and fast before I erupt."

Celia and I had always talked about boys for as long as I could remember. It had all started when we caught Carter making out with a girl in the barn. That incident had sparked thoughts about boys and girls and kissing and groping because Carter had been feeling the girl's breasts. Suddenly, a light bulb came on in my head. That was the reason Carter was so adamant about a boy not getting near me. He knew that a guy would do the same to me. Still, it wasn't for him to decide. If I wanted to make out with a boy, then it was my decision.

"If I know my brother," Emma said, "he won't tell anyone. He's quiet like that. I don't want to hear the details either. I get you two are best friends." She wagged a finger between Celia and me. "But make sure it stays between you two because kids are notorious for taking

S.B. ALEXANDER

things out of context, and before you know it, a kiss has turned into full-blown sex."

I was getting advice from a freshman who seemed older than her fifteen years of age. Nevertheless, she was right. I didn't want Carter and Liam to get wind of Maiken and me. If the rumor spread that Maiken and I had had sex... I didn't want to think about that. My parents would find out, and I would have to explain myself, even if the rumor wasn't true. While that wasn't a big issue, Daddy would look at me weird. I couldn't handle that. I was his little girl. Sure, Maiken and I had only kissed, but Daddy's mind would wander anytime he saw Maiken, especially since Maiken worked for him. That would be bad for both of us.

"I would never tell anyone or put Quinn in a tight spot," Celia said. I imagined she was remembering the rumor she'd started about me.

Emma pressed her pink lips into a thin line. "You sure about that, Celia? Is it true that you hurt Quinn by dumping her to be besties with Tessa? I overheard that in gym class the other day."

Celia hung her head. "I would never do that again." Her tone was filled with sorrow and regret.

A pang of hurt sat heavy on my chest. Sometimes best friends did stupid things. I felt the need to stick up for my bestie. "Don't worry, Emma. What I tell Celia will stay between us." I wasn't one hundred percent sure about that, but Celia deserved a second chance.

A curly black-haired girl wobbled toward us on skates, coming up behind Emma.

Emma raised her fingerless gloved hands as though the curly-haired girl were about to arrest her. "I'm just saying. Keep your make-out sessions with Maiken to yourself."

The girl's eyes got big as she stumbled off the ice, practically falling into Emma. "Who's making out with Maiken?"

Emma whirled around and steadied the girl. "Where did you come from, Dana?"

Celia and I exchanged an amused look. All Emma's advice had just backfired on her. Hopefully, Dana wasn't the type to gossip. Then again, most kids I knew gossiped.

Irony at its finest.

Emma waved at Celia and me then grabbed Dana's hand as the two skated off.

Celia laughed. "Kind of funny that Emma could be responsible for the rumor. You know I wouldn't say a word to anyone."

I was ninety-eight percent sure she wouldn't. Celia and I had built a little trust since we'd made up, but the nagging voice in my head wouldn't let me be completely comfortable. Still, it wasn't as if Maiken and I had gotten naked.

Silence stretched between us while we watched the skaters. Some were giggling, some were breezing around in their own little world, while others fell or bumped into kids in front of them.

"Do you know Dana?" I asked. "Do you think she will spread the rumor?" Worry gripped my belly. I couldn't have a rumor about me floating around school, especially one that involved sex.

"I don't. After what Emma just said, I'm sure she'll talk to Dana." Celia pushed up her glasses higher on her nose. "Now answer me. You believe that I wouldn't spread rumors about you anymore?" She pinned me with a hard look.

If the tables were turned, I would want to hear all about Celia's encounter with a boy. Oh, wait. I had. She'd kissed my brother. But that was all she'd told me. She hadn't given me details such as how my brother kissed. Like Emma, I really didn't want to know about my brother's make-out sessions.

"You promise not to say anything to anyone? My brothers would flip a switch if they heard any rumor about me and Maiken." I held my breath, even though I knew she would promise.

Her cheeks reddened as she frowned. "I'm sorry about spreading the rumor about you at the beginning of school. But you can't hang that over my head forever."

I hooked my arm in hers. "I don't like the attention, Celia. And I don't want to ruin whatever is happening between Maiken and me."

"If anyone is going to ruin you and Maiken, it will be Tessa." She pointed a blue-painted nail at the entrance.

My night just went downhill. I shouldn't have been surprised that Tessa was there. Most of the freshmen and sophomores made the rink their hang-out spot on Saturday nights during the winter.

I didn't get a chance to dwell on Tessa after I laid eyes on the person behind my enemy. Maiken swaggered in, wearing that blue knit hat with his hair sticking out in the front. I loved that hat on him.

Celia bumped her shoulder into mine as I dug my nails into her arm. Good thing she was wearing a thick sweater. Otherwise, I might have drawn blood.

"Swoon," Celia said on a sigh.

Jealousy reared its ugly head. I wanted to shout, "He's mine." But then my gaze came unglued from Maiken and settled on my brother Liam. Both boys towered over Tessa, who flipped her inky-black hair behind her as if she had both boys in the palm of her hand. At that thought, I stiffened even more.

Celia peeled my hand off of her arm. "I love you, Quinn. But I do need my arm."

I let go, balling my hands into fists in my lap.

"Do you want to leave?" Celia asked.

Yes. No. Maybe.

Liam said something in Maiken's ear. Maiken's head turned slowly around the rink as though he were looking for someone, probably Emma. Tessa twirled around and planted her hands on his chest.

I snarled.

Celia did the same. "If she touches Liam, I'm not holding back."

Maiken grinned down at her. My heart sank to the floor, and any ounce of valor I had, which was close to nil, crawled into a hole and died.

I remembered what Emma had said that first day in the hall at school. Maiken was just being polite.

Tessa shimmied her hips closer to him, and I felt as if someone had stomped on my heart with the sharp blade of a skate.

"You should go over there," Celia said.

"I don't want to start trouble." Tessa would eat me alive. "I don't have your courage anyway."

"I promise you. By the end of the school year, if not before, you will have confidence and courage."

"How? Do you have some magic potion?"

Her head bobbed. "Maiken is your magic potion. You stood up to Chase with Maiken at your side. And as the two of you get closer, you'll see."

I spied Emma heading over to her brother with Dana on her tail.

"This should be good," Celia muttered.

Emma said something to Maiken, and then Tessa sneered our way. Maiken's face brightened as he waved.

My heart wasn't on the floor anymore. In fact, it was beating so hard, I was afraid I might have bruised ribs the next day.

Nevertheless, my mind suddenly raced through every moment Maiken and I had spent in the funhouse: the anticipation, my dry mouth, the wild tingles in my belly, his masculine scent, and the thing that had me dreaming about him the night before—his erection, or boner as I'd heard my brothers say. The proper term was phallus or tumescence. *Note to self: Don't spit out facts about an erection in front of Maiken.* I would absolutely die.

"You're turning red," Celia whispered.

That was an understatement. My dreams had been laden with me sitting on top of Maiken while his penis grew. Father Thomas would give me a hefty penance when I went to confession the next day for thinking lewd thoughts about a boy.

But thoughts of confession faded as I worried about the darn rumor. For sure, if Carter and Liam found out about my make-out session with Maiken, they would beat him until he was black and blue. Then he would lose his job. Then I would have to tell them that I was the one who'd had my way with Maiken.

It was more important than ever that I didn't tell Celia anything, even though I was dying to. Considering she liked Liam, she might accidentally tell him.

Celia's voice ended my misery. "Oh, look. Maiken and Liam are coming this way."

But my misery multiplied when Tessa bounced over on Maiken's heels with her hands on him and a look on her face that said he was hers.

In her dreams. The problem was I was all talk in my head. I had to find that courage I so wanted that Celia had promised.

Chapter 22

Maiken

Mr. Thompson had let me off work early since the tree business had slowed during my last hour. I'd protested since I could use the money. But Mr. Thompson had informed me he would pay me for my full shift. I couldn't argue too much with the man. Besides, Liam wanted me to tag along with him to the rink. He'd said the basketball team would be there. Plus, I'd never been to an ice rink before, and I was curious about the venue.

The place was chilly, loud, and had a certain odor I couldn't put my finger on. Aside from that, skaters of all shapes, genders, and sizes glided around the ice. I figuratively scratched my head at how circling a big piece of ice could be fun, although I'd enjoyed watching Quinn on the lake.

As we started for Quinn and Celia, Tessa kept a tight hold on my right arm. *Tell her to bug off,* a small voice in my head prodded. Instead, I gently tugged my arm away. "I need to use the bathroom."

"I'll go with," Liam said in a rush.

I didn't wait to look at Tessa or see her reaction. I practically bolted as fast as I could, not even knowing where the bathroom was located.

Thankfully, Liam led the way.

I'd had girls come up to me at my last school, but none had overtly thrown themselves at me. Those girls had tried to get my attention by talking to me without putting their hands all over me.

As soon as Liam and I were inside, he checked the two stalls. I let out the huge breath I'd been holding.

"We're clear," he said.

I laughed. "Clear from what?" I didn't care if any guys were in the bathroom.

Liam hopped up onto the counter in between two sinks. "I was just making sure Chase wasn't in here."

Even Chase being in the restroom wouldn't have bothered me. I would've welcomed that for sure. I could have used an outlet to relieve some frustration. Maybe he could've helped me by telling his sister to take a hike.

I leaned against a wall not far from Liam. "How many times do I have to tell Tessa that I'm not going to her party?" If she asked me one more time, I might explode.

Liam pulled out his phone from his coat pocket. "She's aggressive. Always has been."

I ran a hand through my hair. "Man, if it's not Chase up my ass, I have to have his sister all over me." It may have been for very different reasons, but either way, I wasn't a Stevens fan.

Liam read something on his phone.

"Are you going?" From the way everyone was talking about the party, I suspected that the whole town would be there.

He typed on his phone. "Celia asked if I could help her mom out that night. You know, her mom is catering the event."

"So what's up with you and Celia anyway?" That day outside the gym, they'd been in a heated discussion.

He set his phone in his lap. "She likes me, but she's my sister's friend and a year younger than me."

"So you're a junior, and she's a sophomore. So what? Do you like her?"

"I'm not into girls who are aggressive," he said. "I like to make the first move."

I harrumphed and cringed at the same time. If he knew that Quinn had made the first move with me, then he might not be too happy. I debated whether to tell him that I liked his sister. Considering how Carter was a crazy man when it came to guys around Quinn, I didn't want to deal with Liam going all nuts too.

"You didn't answer my question. Do you like her?"

He flicked his shaggy brown hair out of his eyes. "Yeah. I think she's cute. I'm not ready to date, though. I got basketball and school."

Boy, did I understand where he was coming from. I needed to get my grades up, or I wouldn't be playing basketball.

"Anyway," he said, "the party is the Saturday before Christmas, and my dad wants Carter and me to be at the Christmas tree stand. Well, if he doesn't sell out by then. You're working that day, right?"

My shift that day started at nine in the morning. "Does he usually sell out of trees?" If he did, then I wouldn't have a job anymore.

Liam jumped down. "Sometimes. The coast is probably clear. Let's go find the team, and I'm hungry too."

I shifted on my feet. "Before we go out there, I wanted to tell you that Coach wants me to play point guard."

He did a double take. "For real? That means Chase gets his way. Fucker. Are you going to?"

"Yes," I said without any hesitation. "I think it would be better. Besides, if I played shooting guard and Chase was point guard, he would never pass the ball to me. Now I'm in control."

"I get the tension between you two, but don't fuck up the game because of him."

I crossed my arms over my chest. "Can he shoot?"

"As I mentioned to you before, he's an okay shooter. Whether you're better than him is still to be determined. No offense."

"It's all good. And not to worry. I'm not a complete ass. I want to win games too." This would be my first game with a new team, and I would be damned if I would screw it up, especially since I was filling a dead boy's shoes. I had to be perfect.

Tessa was waiting outside the men's room.

Holy shit. The woman was relentless.

Liam slapped me on the back. "I'm getting food." Then he ambled toward the food court.

Tessa had her arms folded over her small chest. Yeah, I noticed. I was a schmuck. The town and school were causing me to do things that I hadn't done before like stare at a girl's breasts.

She followed my line of sight, then her red lips slowly parted. "You like, huh?" She closed the short distance between us until she was again too close for my comfort. "We could go somewhere."

I took a step back. "Not happening."

She took a step forward.

We danced this awkward tango until my back was plastered against the wall outside the men's room

The word *fuck* blared in my head. I swallowed a rock as sweat beaded on my neck. "Tessa, do you understand the word no?"

Her hands slid around my waist. "Wow. You really are as toned as I imagined."

I was also tense until a voice, soft and melodic, jolted me.

"M-Maiken," Quinn said in horror.

"Oh my word," Celia added. "Tessa, are you really groping him in public? Figures that you hold true to the slutty rumors about you."

"What's going on here?" a deep male voice asked out of nowhere.

I knew that voice. I hated that voice.

I spotted Chase near Quinn with his head cocked to one side and a scowl on his face. "Sis, are you really touching him?" He sounded disgusted.

"None of your business, brother." Tessa glued her hands to me.

"Maxwell." Chase said my name in warning as though he were trying to scare me, which wasn't working. "I would suggest you move away from my sister."

I rolled my eyes. "Kind of hard to do when I'm pinned to the wall."

Quinn ran up to us. Her big amber eyes had fear floating in them. Nevertheless, she pushed Tessa, who staggered in the direction of her brother.

I could've done what Quinn had, but if I did, then I might have been accused of hurting a girl.

Celia clapped.

My jaw went slack.

When Tessa was steady, she asked in a not-so-nice voice, "Did you just push me, Quinn Thompson? Tell me you didn't."

Quinn stuck up her middle finger.

I grinned like an ass.

In a blur, Tessa ran with her fist primed to punch Quinn. I had little time to think, but Chase beat me to it by grabbing his sister around the waist. "Not today, Tessa."

I gritted my teeth. "'Not today?' Not ever, you mean." I inserted myself in front of Quinn, but she nudged me out of her way. She was braver than I gave her credit for.

"It's inevitable that Tessa and Quinn will duel," Chase said very matter of factly. "You can't stop something that is already planned."

Quinn let out a noise that sounded like a growl. "So you'll let your sister beat me up," she said in a confident tone. "And you want to go out with me? All those nice things you said to me were a lie, then?"

I wanted to kiss her for not stuttering and standing up for herself. I also wanted to hug her because hurt threaded through her last sentence. I didn't like that she felt hurt, and for that, I took one step toward Chase, ready to get in his face, until Tessa stomped on his booted foot.

Chase winced. "Ow. What's that for?"

"You like that pig-smelling girl?" Tessa all but shouted.

I chanced a glance at the rink. Most of the skaters were eyeing us.

Chase's gaze pierced his sister. "What if I do?"

Tessa pursed her lips hard. "Then we're not related."

"I guess we're not then if you like that jerk." Chase stabbed a nubby finger at me.

Celia wormed her way in between Quinn and me. "News flash, Stevens." She took my hand then Quinn's hand and brought them together. "It doesn't matter. These two like each other anyway. So what do you have to say to that?"

Quinn squeezed the hell out of my hand.

Chase grinned like the Cheshire Cat. "Does he know?"

I didn't have to look to know that Chase was pointing his finger at Liam behind me. Still, I checked over my shoulder.

Liam glowered at me. Not Quinn. Me.

Maybe it was time to move south.

Before I could say a word, Liam grabbed my arm and all but dragged me into the boys' restroom.

Quinn tried to stop her brother while the Stevens siblings laughed.

"Let them go," Celia said to Quinn.

Once inside, Liam paced furiously, running his hands through his hair. "If my father finds out, he'll fire you."

Okay, that wasn't what I was expecting to hear. I was ready for him to throw a punch or tackle me to the floor.

"Your dad knows I like Quinn."

He stopped short, almost falling forward. "Say again? My dad?"

"Yep. Look, I like your sister. I'm not going to hide that anymore. So if you want a go at me, now is the time. I'll give you one punch. Then get over it. She can make decisions for herself."

The fight drained from him. "Nah. I'm not going to. Carter might. But if you so much as hurt her in any way, I will take you up on that punch."

I raised my hands. "Deal." Two of the Thompson men were out of the way. Well, maybe Mr. Thompson wasn't yet. He knew I liked his daughter, but seeing us together might be a different story. And Carter would be harder to convince.

Liam sighed. "I'm just glad she has no interest in Chase."

"Agree, man." Chase could still be a problem, and it wasn't as though Quinn and I were officially dating.

The door squeaked open, and Quinn came in. "Both you and Carter need to stay out of my business."

"I'm cool," Liam said.

Her little nose scrunched. "Huh?"

Liam stabbed his thumb at me. "I like him. Plus, he knows where I stand."

She rolled her eyes. "Yeah, a fist away from getting his nose broken if he hurts me. Right?"

The door opened again, and Celia peeked in. "Everything okay in here?"

Liam's hard features slackened when he locked eyes with Celia.

My phone rang.

"Maiken," Ethan said. "Where are you? You need to get home." His tone sent a chill down my spine.

"What happened?"

"Harlan is missing. Get home now!"

My stomach balled into one big knot. "On my way."

Liam touched my arm. "We could hear your brother's voice through the phone. Let's get you home."

The color drained from Quinn's face. Hell, my face had to be white. The temperatures were zero or below, and if Harlan was missing, that meant... I didn't want to think that far ahead.

Chapter 23

Quinn

L iam sped through the streets of Ashford as Maiken fidgeted in the passenger seat. Sitting behind Liam, I could see part of Maiken's anguish. His body was as hard as a stone.

"Do you know where he would go?" Liam asked.

Maiken shook his head profusely. "He loves the outdoors. He could be anywhere." He tapped on his phone before lifting it to his ear. "With the temperatures dropping... Fuck. My mom must be going nuts. Sorry, I didn't mean to swear."

Liam chuckled. "Fuck is right."

Momma and Daddy didn't like to hear anyone saying that word. But kids at school said it frequently. I'd come to the conclusion that swearing was a rite of passage for teenagers, particularly those who couldn't say the word in the company of their parents.

Regardless, I was biting my nails. Maiken was right. The temperature wasn't in Harlan's favor.

"Carter and my dad are meeting us at the Maxwells' with the snowmobiles," Liam said. "They know the woods surrounding the town quite well. They'll find him." He'd called Daddy as soon as we'd gotten in the car, and if anyone knew the terrain in Ashford, it was Daddy. He'd grown up in that town and knew every nook and cranny the town had.

"Any luck, Ethan?" Maiken hung his head. "What? You're kidding me. Yeah, Liam called his dad. How's Mom? We're almost there." He lowered the phone. "My brothers, Marcus and Jasper, were supposed to be watching Harlan. But they were playing foosball and not paying attention to Harlan." He muttered something under his breath.

I didn't want to think that maybe Harlan had fallen through the ice. When I'd skated on it the day before, the ice was solid, and with the continued cold temps, the ice would only get thicker. Still, that didn't mean there wasn't a weak spot somewhere along the shore.

Liam and I exchanged a knowing look as though he'd had the same thought.

Maiken turned slightly. "Quinn, the ice was good when you were on it yesterday. Right?"

The fear written all over his face made my heart sputter. "It was."

Liam wheeled down the dark two-lane road leading up to the Maxwell's.

"He's not in the lake," Liam blurted out. "If anything, he probably wandered off on one of the trails. Carter and I did that all the time on the trails around the farm when we were kids."

"Our mom would pull her hair out," I added.

"My mom is freaking out," Maiken said.

Cars dotted the Maxwell's driveway, including Daddy's truck, complete with the massive trailer that he used to haul the snowmobiles. Liam barely came to a stop behind Daddy's truck when Maiken flew out.

The property was lit up like a football stadium with spotlights shining on all sides including the backyard around the lake.

I waited for Liam to turn off his truck before I got out. Harlan's name could be heard over the distant whir of snowmobiles.

Maiken ran into the house. Liam and I wound our way around the garage.

"He probably saw a deer or a rabbit," Liam said. "Remember the time Carter and I saw a rabbit along the edge of the farm." He laughed. "We were determined to capture it that night."

"Yeah, but that was a hot summer night and not around a lake in the winter," I reminded him as I crossed my fingers inside my gloves, praying for Harlan.

Daddy emerged through the trees, bundled up in his snowmobile gear. Carter came up behind him. But there was no sign of Harlan.

Before I knew what was happening, a woman ran down, screaming, "Where is he?" I suspected she was Maiken's mom.

Daddy cut the engine on his snowmobile, as did Carter.

"Kade has him," Daddy said.

Liam caught the lady before she collapsed on the snow.

Daddy rushed to her side, taking off his jacket. "He's okay." He draped his coat over her.

Lights bounced beyond us before Kade appeared with the shivering curly-haired little boy.

The entire Maxwell family converged down by the lake. Well, except for Mr. Maxwell. I didn't see him.

Maiken's siblings shouted and screamed.

Maiken's mom pulled Harlan from Kade, kissing him and touching him as though she were looking for cuts and bruises. "Harlan Maxwell." Her tone was motherly. "Never mind. We'll talk about this later."

Maiken joined his mom. "I'll take him up to the house."

A little girl with blackish-brown hair ran up to Maiken and Harlan then punched Harlan in the arm. "You're not supposed to go out by yourself."

Laughter erupted.

Eleanor Maxwell thanked Daddy and Carter then hugged Kade.

I leaned into Liam. "I'm going up to the house with Maiken."

I didn't get far, though.

"Quinn," Daddy said. "It's late. Let's go home." I knew he meant that we should let the family have their quiet time. As much as I wanted to go with Maiken, I couldn't disobey Daddy.

"Carter and Liam, get the snowmobiles up on the trailer," Daddy ordered.

Like me, my brothers didn't talk back. They readied the snowmobiles, and the engines fired to life before they drove away.

Maiken's mom corralled her children. "It's freezing out here. Emma and Ethan, help the kids into the house."

I wanted to introduce myself to Maiken's mom, but Daddy's raised brow told me to get moving.

As if Maiken's mom was in my head, she came up to me. "Quinn, we haven't officially met. I'm Christine, Maiken's mom. So you're the girl who's snagged Maiken's attention?"

Daddy didn't even flinch, which was odd. I would've thought he would groan or sneer or something.

All I could do was nod at her.

Then she addressed Daddy. "I can't thank you and your son enough for helping Kade search for Harlan."

"Please, call me Jeff. And you're more than welcome." Daddy was so sweet. Then again, I knew he was. He would help anyone if they needed it.

All of us made our way to the garage.

Kade and Daddy walked behind Eleanor, Christine, and me, talking about the house Kade was building.

Eleanor adjusted the furry red scarf around her neck. "I hear you're going to the Stevenses' party with Chase Stevens."

"He asked me, but I declined," I said.

"Quinn, Mrs. Stevens has invited Martin, me, my boys, and their wives," Eleanor said. "Well, Kelton and Kody aren't married yet. Anyway, your mom told me you really want to go. Kross and Kelton can't make it. So that leaves four open invitations. Why don't you and Maiken tag along with Martin and me?"

"That would be good for Maiken to meet more people," Christine added.

I wasn't sure it would be good for Maiken or me. If we showed up together, which I was all for, I knew Tessa would throw a temper tantrum and make a spectacle out of me. Even if she didn't, she would try to get her nasty hands on Maiken for sure. On top of all that, Chase wouldn't take kindly to me showing up with Maiken.

When we walked around the garage, Liam and Carter were closing the door to the trailer.

"Think about it, Quinn," Eleanor said. "Martin and I would love for you to join us."

Christine handed Daddy his coat. "Thanks again."

Eleanor and Christine said their goodbyes, and as they were going in, Maiken was coming out.

"How's Harlan?" I asked Maiken.

He zipped up his jacket. "Cold. Still scared. I know my mom thanked you, Mr. Thompson, but I want to do the same. You too, Carter."

Carter nodded from the Daddy's truck with no scowl or meanness emanating from him.

Interesting.

Daddy put on his coat. ""Boys, take my truck. I'll drive Liam's."

Liam tossed Daddy his keys.

Carter hesitated a moment, regarding me then Maiken.

I wanted to roll my eyes. He wasn't the patriarch of the family.

When my brothers were finally backing out of the driveway, Kade asked, "Jeff, could you take a look at our tractor while you're here? It would only take a few minutes. We've been having problems with the engine."

Daddy knew tractors like I knew random facts. "Sure."

They went into the garage through the side door, leaving Maiken and me alone in the driveway.

Now what?

"So your aunt wants us to go the Stevenses' p-party with her and y-your uncle."

"That's weird," he said.

I didn't want to assume anything in those two words, but I couldn't help but wonder if he thought us going together was weird. Maybe it was, considering we would be attending a party given by our enemies. At that thought, I laughed.

He moistened his lips with his tongue. "Weird, right? That we would go together to Tessa and Chase's party?"

I wanted to ask if he would go, but I didn't want to come off as aggressive like Tessa. At the rink, I could tell Maiken was suffocating with Tessa breathing down his neck.

"Are you going to go, then?" he asked.

I shrugged. "Are you?"

"Nah. I'm not into parties," he said.

I held in a frown until he did the one thing I'd been wishing he would do since the funhouse—he kissed me, sweetly and tenderly. Any notion of parties vanished.

Chapter 24

Maiken

I kicked the covers off me, sweating like a pig. When I tried to lift my head, I cringed at the pain. I turned in bed to find my body achy and my sheets wet.

Ugh! I couldn't get sick. I had to work, plus I had practice and school all next week.

I blinked a few times to clear the sleep from my eyes. Ethan's bed was empty, and the clock on our nightstand read seven a.m. Ethan usually slept in on weekends until noon.

Maybe it wasn't Sunday, and I was supposed to be in school. I rifled through my memory of the events of the day before.

Harlan!

I sat straight up. I'd never been so flipping scared in all my life. When Ethan had told me that Harlan was missing, I couldn't breathe, especially when I thought of the cold, the dark, the frozen lake, and the woods. None of that was comforting for a seven-year-old. I would've died if we'd lost Harlan. I understood Mom's concern over the kids being down by the lake without supervision more than ever now. Not that I didn't before, but we'd never lived in the cold or snow or around a lake. Sure, we'd all taken swimming lessons as kids, but with the temperatures of the lake water at this time of year, no amount of swimming lessons would save anyone, particularly a seven-year-old.

I was sure from there on out, Mom wasn't about to let Harlan out of her sight. She'd reprimanded Marcus and Jasper then grounded them from the funhouse until spring. They'd argued, but Mom was tougher on her discipline than Dad had been at times.

Mom glided into my room, wearing a sweater dress and boots with a silk scarf draped around her neck. Her smile told me she was in a better mood. "You're awake. You need to get ready for church."

"Since when do we go to church?" The last time I'd seen the inside of one had been at Dad's funeral.

She disappeared into the closet. "Your aunt and uncle go to church every Sunday, and we should too. Listening to the priest's sermon might give us all perspective on life." She emerged with a pair of my only dress pants and a white button-up shirt. "I hear Quinn might be at church. Aunt Eleanor says the Thompsons are there every Sunday."

Hearing Quinn's name had always elicited some kind of stomach reaction or an extra beat of my heart, but that morning, I didn't get one sign. I chalked that up to how achy I felt. Then I remembered I'd kissed Quinn. That meant she was probably sick too.

Flopping back onto the pillow, I rubbed my eyes. "I'm not feeling so well."

Mom deposited my clothes on the edge of my bed then felt my forehead. "Oh no. You're burning up." Her motherly tone wrapped around me—soothing and comforting. "I'll be right back. I'm going to get a thermometer."

She didn't need one as hot and sweaty as I was. Not to mention, the act of swallowing was painful. I curled into a ball.

Mom returned and placed the thermometer into my mouth before I could protest. "I hate this cold weather. It's going to be a long winter." She sat down on the bed. "All of you will be sick now."

She was right. When one kid got sick, the rest of us followed, including her.

Within a couple of minutes, the thermometer beeped. Removing it, she arched a brow, shaking her head. "It's 101, bordering on 102. I'll see if Aunt Eleanor has any medicine."

"Mom, how's Harlan?" I'd had a hard time falling asleep the night before, thinking about how scared Harlan had been when I'd brought him into the house.

"Why did you take off like that?" I'd asked him.

"I saw a deer through the window in the house on the water," he'd replied.

"Buddy, you can't take off like that. Ever," I'd said in a stern tone. "Do you hear me?"

He'd nodded as he cried.

My heart had skipped several beats as I'd held him to me tightly.

Mom's hand cupped my face. "He's bragging how he chased a deer." She rose, shaking her head. "All of you have had your moments, but none of you have ever taken off. If your father were here, he would've cut down every tree until he found Harlan. Still, Kade and the Thompson family jumped into action faster than I expected."

"Where was Uncle Martin?" I hadn't seen him, and it didn't matter now, but he could've reacted much faster than anyone if he'd been there.

"He had a business dinner. I'll be right back."

Mom brushed shoulders with Ethan as he strutted in, wearing his Sunday best. His hair was slicked back too, which was odd since he hardly combed his hair.

"You're wondering why my hair looks like this," he said.

I coughed. "It crossed my mind. Listen, you should get out before you get sick. I probably have the flu."

He shrugged. "What does it matter? I have to sleep in this room. As long as you don't cough or sneeze on me, I should be cool." He was the bravest out of all us brothers. "So you're not working today, then?"

I couldn't even think about work let alone move without feeling yucky. "I'll have Mom call Mr. Thompson."

He sat on his bed, facing me. "So how's Quinn?" He waggled his eyebrows, wanting details.

I pushed myself up until I was resting against the headboard. "You're enjoying seeing me with a girl?"

"Hell yeah. Do you need some advice?"

I broke out in laughter then coughed. "Quinn and I kissed." I could tell Ethan anything, and he wouldn't spread rumors or say a word. That was our brotherly code.

Actually, Emma fell into that group with Ethan and me. We didn't like rumors. Luckily, we hadn't been the center of attention at prior schools. There was always some kid or group more in the spotlight than us. Then again, most times we weren't at a school long enough for anyone to spread rumors about us anyway, although that was changing.

I'd only been at Kensington a week—one damn week—and I was already the center of attention with Tessa and Chase.

No one other than Ethan and Emma could know about Quinn and me kissing. The blood drained from me just thinking about what Carter could do to me. At least I had Liam in my corner, and maybe even Mr. Thompson.

Ethan smirked. "How was your first kiss?"

I hiked a shoulder, or maybe the chill coursing through me made me react. "Okay." *Liar.* It was explosive in more ways than one.

"Did you get a boner?" Ethan asked seriously.

I snorted. "What do you think?"

"I always do," he said, his gaze on something on the other side of the room as though he were remembering his first time. "It's natural, right?"

For sure. "Quinn noticed my boner too."

He gave me a cheeky grin. "Girls aren't as innocent as you think."

It was my turn to grin. "I wouldn't know. Remember, I haven't had girlfriends."

"Do you want to kiss her again?"

In a heartbeat. "Hell yeah."

"If you two go out, won't that affect your job?" Ethan asked.

"My job ends the day before Christmas." I only had twenty-two more days of work. I'd been counting only to calculate how much money I would make in the time I had left.

"You should probably wait until your jobs ends before you ask her on a date," Ethan said. "Remember those stories we heard Dad telling Mom about coworkers getting caught dating?"

Mom returned. "Ethan, out. You should sleep in the family room tonight."

Ethan got up. "I'll be fine in my bed. Talk to you later, bro." Then he was gone.

My mom handed me a glass of water and two pills. "After church, I'll stop and get some better medicine. Aunt Eleanor only had Advil. I'll also make some soup when I get back."

I chased down the two green pills with water.

Mom sat on the edge of the bed. "Maiken, Aunt Eleanor invited Quinn to go to the Stevenses' party, and she has an invitation for you too."

"I know. Quinn told me. I'm not going."

"I thought you liked Quinn."

All the pretty girls in the world couldn't get me to budge on my decision. And the more people that talked or gushed about the damn Stevenses' party, the more I was ready to scream. "It's a party for rich folks. We don't fall into that category." We never had. Even if we did, we wouldn't flaunt our status around like Tessa seemed to do.

"Maiken, we don't need to be well off to attend a party. You should consider the invitation if for nothing else than to spend some time with your aunt and uncle. I hear Kade and his wife are going too."

"You go, Mom. I'll babysit."

She cupped one side of my cheek with her cold hand. "You're sweet. But I'll babysit, and I'll be baking that night anyway."

My eyes went wide. "Your famous Christmas cookies?"

"You betcha. Emma wants to go, but she wasn't invited," Mom said.

In a roundabout way, she had been when Tessa had invited me. "She should go in my place, then."

Mom studied me with soft brown eyes, almost sad. "Please think about it. I want you to make new friends. Have a good time. It will take your mind off of your father."

Nothing would ever take my mind away from Dad. Well, maybe there was one person who could, but right then I wanted to sleep and nothing more. "I have to work that day."

"I'm sure Mr. Thompson would understand." She rose. "Rest."

"Mom, say a prayer for Dad while you're in church." Instantly, tears filled my eyes.

She left me with the saddest of smiles I'd ever seen on my mom, and because of that, I buried my head in my pillow and cried.

Chapter 25

Quinn

Sunday mass was the same routine every week. We got up early and dressed in our Sunday best. I rode with Momma and Daddy while Carter and Liam drove in Carter's truck. We sat in the same pew. The parishioners knew not to take our spot three rows behind the first on the left. Like any week, the liturgical aroma floated in the air and always gave me the feeling that I was somewhere other than in a church. Momma didn't like the smell of frankincense and myrrh, but Daddy did because he said it calmed his mind.

After he'd made that statement many years ago, I'd been curious about the word itself, which had made me giggle. Even Celia had snorted when she heard the word.

"The frankincense comes from a Boswellia tree from somewhere far away," I'd told Celia.

She'd made a weird face. "It sounds like something from a Frankenstein movie."

I smiled at the memory, watching the altar boys prepare the pulpit for Father Thomas. Carter and Liam had been altar boys until their confirmation in the Catholic Church. I'd never been an altar girl, although Father Thomas had had two girls in the ranks a few years ago.

Momma read from the weekly church bulletin while Daddy stared straight ahead. Boredom always set in while we waited for mass to begin. I dared not take out my phone, or Daddy would stomp on it like he had when Liam had texted one of his friends one Sunday morning.

I checked on my brothers. Carter was on my left, bouncing his knee. Liam was on the other side of Carter, picking at a scab on his hand. My brothers looked so handsome in their pressed shirts and slacks.

The rustling of clothes and coats and whispers echoed off the stained-glass windows and candlelit walls. High above and behind me, Mrs. Dannon played the organ. The sound competed with the incoming parishioners.

Momma placed a gentle hand on my knee. "Stop fidgeting."

I hadn't realized I was mimicking Carter. I smoothed a hand down my leggings. With the cold weather, I didn't wear dresses on Sundays. Momma did, though. That day, she wore a black dress that was cinched at the waist with a cranberry-colored belt, and a gray silk scarf flowed around her neck.

Daddy held Momma's hand as he eyed me around Momma. He was just as handsome as my brothers. Sunday was the only day I got to see Daddy in his nice wool pants, shiny shoes, and crisp cotton shirt.

I gave Daddy a big smile. He winked then sat back. Daddy was a hard man, but he had a heart of gold when it came to his family. I knew Carter and Liam took after Daddy in many ways including their belief that boys should stay far away from me. But Carter seemed to be the one who really hated the idea of me dating, although I hadn't broached the topic with Daddy.

I tapped Carter on his thigh. "Can I talk to you after church?" Liam had come around about Maiken and me, although we weren't exactly dating. Regardless, I wanted to test the subject with Carter and get the elephant out of the room.

"Make it quick," Carter said in a gruff voice. "Liam and I have somewhere to go." His tone was short as always.

I knew that *somewhere* they were going. Every Sunday after mass, Carter and Liam trekked off to the shooting range in town. I wasn't allowed to go, even though I'd tried many times to convince them to take me along.

"Guns aren't for girls," Carter had said many times.

"It's our bro time," Liam had added.

I'd accepted Liam's statement over Carter's. I'd understood the brotherly relationship, but that didn't make them not wanting me around any easier. That was about the time Momma had taken me skating at the rink. After that, I'd found something I was good at. So I didn't bother my brothers anymore. Besides, I'd only wanted to spend time with them, not shoot guns. Daddy had shown me how to shoot a BB gun anyway. That had satisfied my curiosity.

I checked the time on my phone. Mass was about to start.

"I wonder if Eleanor is coming today," Momma said almost to herself.

"She invited me to go with her and Mr. Maxwell to the Stevenses' party," I said in a whisper to Momma.

She patted my leg, her glossy nails glistening in the light. "I know. She told me she was going to ask you." Her pink-stained lips split into a slow smile. "I hear she wants Maiken to go too."

Just as I was about to respond, Eleanor and Martin walked up. Martin nodded to us as Eleanor beamed. She was as beautiful as ever in her royal-blue dress, which brought out her stunning blue eyes. She slid into the pew in front of us, which was their normal seat for mass. Martin stood like a soldier, his honey-colored eyes fixated on something toward the back of the church.

Butterflies held steady in my stomach as I wished upon a star that Maiken was walking down the aisle, even though he hadn't been to church since he'd moved there.

The swarm of butterflies went back to sleep when Christine glided up, her brown hair poking out of a crocheted white hat as she held onto Harlan's hand. The little tike seemed to be fine after his ordeal in the woods. He resembled his mom with a small nose and brown eyes. Behind Christine was Ethan. There was no mistaking the fact that Ethan and Harlan were brothers. Nevertheless, if Ethan was there, then maybe Maiken was too. I glanced over my shoulder and frowned.

As if Ethan knew where my mind was going, he said, "Maiken has the flu."

Oh, no. We'd kissed the night before, but I didn't feel sick.

Daddy finally spoke. "Will he be at work later?"

Christine sat next to Eleanor. "I'm sorry, Jeff. He's got a 102 fever."

Momma winced.

"So he won't be in school tomorrow?" Liam asked.

Ethan sat down in between Harlan and Martin. "Sorry, dude. I don't think so."

"We need him for basketball practice," Liam muttered.

Daddy needed Maiken for work. Liam needed him for basketball, and I just needed him for no other reason than to make out. Celia had been right. Boys were everything, or one in particular was to me anyway.

Father Thomas walked out from a side door with the altar boys in tow. That was our cue to rise. Forty-five minutes later, after praying, singing, taking communion, and listening to Father Thomas's sermon on giving during the holiday season, we slowly made our way out of church.

During mass, all I'd thought about was Maiken. I should bring him some soup or maybe some of the coffee rolls Momma had baked that morning.

"Boys," Daddy said to my brothers. "I need you at the Christmas tree stand by one today."

Carter and Liam didn't appear happy, but they nodded just the same.

Ethan tapped Daddy on the shoulder. "Mr. Thompson, I can work in Maiken's place. I'm not sixteen yet, though."

Daddy considered Ethan as we gathered outside. "You don't mind? I could use you. Can you come at one this afternoon?"

Ethan nodded while Carter and Liam lost their cranky attitudes. I didn't blame my brothers for getting annoyed. All of us worked hard on the farm, especially during the holiday season. They deserved one day to goof off.

"I can help too," I said to Daddy. I hadn't planned on working the tree stand. I had homework and chores in the house, but Momma would understand.

Daddy gave me one of his warm grins that told me he was proud.

Eleanor, Christine, and Momma chatted where the stone steps met the sidewalk.

Fluffy clouds floated overhead. Kade and his beautiful wife, Lacey, leaned against a shiny blue truck not far from where we stood. Lacey was all bundled up and tucked into Kade's side.

The last time I'd seen her was in the local grocery store months ago when I was shopping with Momma. Her long, wavy brown hair had been up in a ponytail at that time instead of cascading down her back like it was that day.

While Momma and Daddy talked with Christine, Eleanor, and Martin, I decided to talk to Carter before he and Liam took off. But when I glanced around, I didn't see my brother until a family of five walked past me.

What in the world? Carter and Chase seemed as though they were in a heated discussion about five cars down, near a tree.

"Quinn," Lacey called.

I pursed my lips, ready to stomp over to Chase and my brother, but I couldn't be rude. "Yes, ma'am."

She and Kade held hands. "You're right," she said to Kade. "Kade tells me that you've snagged Maiken's attention. I see why. You're beautiful."

She was talking to me as if she'd never met me. While I wanted to remind her that we had met briefly a time or two, I couldn't let Carter leave. Not only that, I was dying to know what Chase was babbling to him about.

Lacey must've seen some type of expression cross my face because she said, "Forgive me. I didn't mean that to come out as though we don't know each other. Well, we really don't. I've never had a chance to talk to you or get to know you."

I didn't expect to be friends with Lacey. She was much older than me. Besides, she was hardly in town during baseball season. My brothers gushed about how she played for a men's team.

"If you'll forgive me, I need to talk to my brother before he leaves."

"Quite all right," Lacey said. "I hope to see you at the Stevenses' party. Maybe we can chat then."

Maiken wasn't going, but I hadn't thought about my answer yet. I hated to be rude and decline Eleanor's invitation. After all, she and Momma knew I wanted to go.

"Maybe," I said. "Excuse me." My mind wasn't on anything else except Chase and Carter at that moment. As I approached Carter and Chase, I scanned the church grounds for Tessa. She had to be there if Chase was. But I came up empty. "So are you talking about me?" I asked without stuttering.

Chase wore a cold expression and all but scurried away like a rat in a sewer.

"What's going on?" I asked Carter.

Steam came out of Carter's nose and not because of the cold. "There's a rumor going around that Maiken got in your pants."

Blood froze in my veins as a ball of fur clogged my throat.

Liam jogged up, maybe because he'd seen the fury on Carter's face.

"Well?" Carter asked in a tone that lifted the fine hairs on the back of my neck.

My worst possible fear had come to fruition. I couldn't even think clearly or get my tongue to move.

"Care to fill me in?" Liam asked.

"Do you know about Maiken getting into our sister's pants?" Carter almost growled every world.

Liam flinched. "Bull. Quinn wouldn't let that happen."

A small part of me relaxed that I had at least one brother who believed I would save my virtue for the right boy. Nevertheless, Liam eyed me, wanting me to confirm what he'd said.

I swished some saliva around in my mouth. "You know something, Carter? You're worse than Daddy." Holding back tears, I started to head back to my parents. I couldn't talk to my brother right then. Not to mention, that rumor would spread like wildfire around school, and all eyes would be on me. Girls would giggle in groups. Boys would size me up. And Tessa... Oh, she would have a field day with me for sure.

Carter skirted around me, looking down. "Is it true?"

I loved my brother, but at that moment, I despised him for the mere fact that he would believe a rumor about me.

Liam was right next to Carter, seemingly ready to intervene if he had to.

My lips trembled. "Did you believe the rumor that Celia and Tessa spread around about me?"

"Of course not."

"Then why would you even think to believe this one? And consider the source." I believed Chase had been sincere when he'd said he liked me. But maybe he was mad after learning that I liked Maiken. Maybe this was his way of getting back at Maiken or me.

"Because I see the way you look at Maiken," Carter said, not losing an ounce of anger.

I gulped, the cold air cooling the burn in the back of my throat. "Stay out of my business." I stomped away, desperate to get home and hide in the loft, where I could think, cry, and never show my face again in school.

Chapter 26

Maiken

Three days out of school. Three days of missed basketball practice. Three days of feeling as if someone had zapped all the energy out of me. But nothing was worse than when Emma had charged into my bedroom after school on Monday, babbling about some rumor that Quinn and I had slept together.

As I closed my locker, I searched up and down the halls for Quinn. Emma had said she hadn't seen Quinn all week.

Ethan nudged my shoulder. "I don't see Quinn."

"I don't understand how you're not sick," I said. Emma had the flu now, but Ethan was the one sharing a room with me.

He shrugged. "Can't answer that, bro. So what are you going to do about the rumor? You truly didn't have sex with her?"

Narrowing my eyes at my brother, I leaned into him and whispered, "When I lose my virginity, you'll be the first to know."

He chuckled. "I can't wait for that day. Look, Emma and I haven't seen Quinn. I didn't even see her when I filled in for you at the tree farm last Sunday. Even then, Liam and Carter didn't say anything to me, although Carter wasn't around much."

"How was Liam?" I didn't forget his threat to throw that punch if I hurt his sister, and while I didn't, the rumor was rather jarring. If I'd heard that rumor about Emma I would probably be livid.

Ethan threaded his fingers through his messy hair. "He seemed fine, and no, he didn't say anything to me. I got to run. Don't forget to see Coach during your free period. I hear he's been looking for you."

The bell rang.

Ethan went one way, and I went the other. I didn't get far when Tessa popped out from around the corner at the end of the hall. I could only go left, so there was no way to avoid her. I ground my back teeth together.

She clutched a book in her arms. "Is it true? Please tell me it isn't." She sounded as though she'd lost her chance with me. I was on the verge of telling her she'd never had a chance when Carter of all people marched my way with his fists ready for battle.

A handful of kids lingered.

Tessa flipped her hair over her shoulder along with a quick glance. "He doesn't seem happy."

"You started the rumor, didn't you?" I asked through gritted teeth.

She gave me a smug smile. "Why would I do that when I like you?"

I couldn't argue with her on that point, and she did seem all doom and gloom. "Maybe it was your brother, then?" I recalled Ethan telling me he'd seen Chase talking to Carter after church.

She rolled her dark eyes. "Seriously? Chase likes Quinn. Why? I don't know. But again, that would be the last thing Chase would do. It wasn't us."

I didn't get a chance to question her further.

Carter's nostrils flared as he got nearer. "Tessa, leave us."

"Good luck." Tessa hurried off.

Carter growled at those lingering. "Get out of here."

They scattered like cockroaches.

In a flash, Carter's fist landed with a *thwack* on my nose.

I saw stars as anger, hot and sticky, shot forward. "Fuck." I was a second away from throwing my own punch.

A muscle jumped in his jaw. "Don't even try to hit me. And if you go near my sister again, you'll have more than a bloody nose." He started to walk away.

Like hell. He wasn't dismissing me. The only people who could do that were my parents. I latched onto his shoulder. He was as tall as me, but he was way bigger in the chest, and he packed a whopping punch.

He spun on his heel, eyeing my hand then my face. "You got some balls touching me."

I couldn't help the laugh that burst free as blood trickled from my nose and into my mouth. "Do you want the truth? Or do you want to get all up in my face over a rumor that isn't true?"

"It is true," he said.

I laughed again. "You know this how?" I had to hear his reasoning.

"My sister didn't deny it."

I traded his shoulder for the strap of my backpack. "So she told you we had sex?"

He winced at the last word. "No. Look, Quinn is easy to take advantage of. So stay away from her."

Spikes of anger jabbed my gut. "Not happening unless Quinn tells me to."

He took one step, and we were nose to nose. "I'm telling you."

My nostrils pulsated even as the blood oozed out. "Did you tell Chase Stevens the same thing? Wait, he was the one who told you that rumor." I wasn't certain of that.

Carter created distance between us. "He was only watching out for Quinn. Remember what I said." He turned the corner.

I was going to level Chase. If he wanted to play dirty, I could too.

A creaking door echoed in the hallway before a soft voice said, "Don't pay him any attention."

I turned and found Quinn looking pale and sad as she held on to the door of the girls' restroom.

As I drew closer, she waved me off. "I think I have the flu. S-so don't come any closer."

I guess I shouldn't have been surprised since we'd swapped spit.

She raked her gaze over me. "Carter hit you?"

I dragged my fingers under my nose. "It's nothing." The blood was beginning to dry around my nose.

She pointed her small finger at my right eye. "It looks like you might have a black eye."

"Were you listening long?" I asked.

"Only the last bit. But I knew he was going to say something to you." Her skin was ashen.

"Are you going home?" I didn't want to talk in the hall or anywhere at school. "I can take you." I had the family car since Mom didn't need it.

"I w-was going to call my mom. But you should get to class." She batted her long lashes at me.

I would carry her in my arms if I had to. *Wait. Where did that come from?* "I'm already lagging behind on my classes. One or two more isn't going to make a difference. Besides, the teachers aren't expecting me since I've been out sick."

A pained expression washed over her, and I couldn't tell if that was because she wasn't feeling well or because of what I'd just said.

"Come on. I'll drive you home." It would give me a chance to spend time with her. All I'd thought about when I was lying in bed was Quinn.

Chapter 27

Quinn

The Suburban bounced over the road, making me queasier than I already was. My body was prickly and achy. My brain felt the same way. It had been a rough week with the rumor going around school about Maiken and me having sex. I had turned red from embarrassment whenever kids whispered or looked my way. I knew what I had been in for walking into school on that Monday morning. Even now that Thursday had rolled around, the whispers were still there.

Celia kept telling me to ignore the gossipers and the looks and Tessa, but I wasn't one to easily ignore anything. I had gotten a reprieve when I'd first seen Tessa at her locker. She'd given me a look of disgust, rolled her eyes, and stomped off as though she hadn't gotten her way. I expected her to retaliate in some fashion. Still, I had done my best to avoid her because when the shock or whatever it was that she was feeling wore off, I would be more than her pincushion. I would become her punching bag.

Even still, I'd been tempted to change up her little rhyme about me from "Quinn, Quinn will never win. You'll never get the boy." to "Quinn, Quinn did win. I did get the boy." But I wasn't a harridan like her and didn't want to be either.

Maiken was deep in thought as he drove. I glanced out at the snow-covered landscape as homes clipped by on the two-lane country road.

"Did Chase start that rumor?" Maiken's voice crackled as though he needed to clear his throat.

For days, I'd racked my brain trying to figure out who would say such a thing. Chase had motive—he wanted me. Tessa had one too—she wanted Maiken. What better way to separate the two of us than by telling Carter? Chase knew my brother would pop a vein. Rumor aside, it hurt that my own blood believed such hearsay. Sure, Carter wasn't wrong when he'd said, "I see the way you look at him." But that didn't mean I would give away my virtue so easily. Momma and Daddy had taught us to respect ourselves and protect the precious things about who we were.

"One day, when you're ready, you'll want to have relations with a boy," Momma had counseled me when I'd first gotten my monthly friend. "And when that time comes, I want you to promise me that you'll come to me first, but I also want you to make darn sure it's a boy you really want to give your virginity to."

Oh my God. I wasn't ready to have sex. I was just learning how to kiss.

"Quinn?" Maiken said. "Where did you go?"

I blinked. "I h-hate being the c-center of attention."

He focused on the road. "Rumors suck."

"What's w-worse is Carter believes the rumor."

He pointed to his nose. "I know."

"Your eye is starting to color."

He glanced in the rearview mirror. "It shouldn't be too bad. So, do you think Chase or Tessa started it?"

"I'm almost positive Tessa didn't. Not sure about Chase." I hadn't seen him at school. He wasn't in any of my classes since he was a junior. At lunch, I'd gone to the library instead of the cafeteria.

"Carter didn't tell you?" he asked.

I'd been avoiding my brother, and when we were at dinner or in the barn, we didn't speak. Or rather, I hadn't said a word to Carter. I was still angry with him. "No." But it was time to have a talk with my brother and somehow make him understand that he couldn't control my life. "I'll talk to him." Better yet, if I had Daddy's approval to date, then Carter might not be so over-the-top brotherly.

Maiken's knuckles were white as he gripped the steering wheel. "Give him some time. He needs to cool off now that he took out his anger on me, although he isn't going to like that I drove you home. But I really don't care."

His last line made my heart swell as big as the Atlantic Ocean. Most boys ran when they saw Carter talking to me.

"You know I would never disrespect you," Maiken said.

I gave him a weak smile, only because I wasn't feeling well. "I know. It doesn't matter who started it. It's not like we're going to have them make an announcement saying that they lied." That would be wonderful, though, mainly to get Carter to settle down.

He slid his hand over the console and turned up his palm. "Give me your hand."

"You're g-going to get sick again."

"So?"

I placed my palm on his, and my pulse rioted, waking up the dormant butterflies inside my belly.

"I was just thinking. Why don't we give everyone something truthful to talk about?"

I swallowed over a lump. I didn't want anyone talking about me. *Tessa is the only one that makes your days in school miserable. Why not give her something else to shut her up?* That depended on what he had in mind. I was afraid to ask but excited at the same time. So I took in a deep breath. "What do you have in mind?"

"Be *my* girl." He emphasized the word *my* with a grin that was all kinds of swoony and tingling.

Those three words were better than *I love you.* "Um... Um. O-okay." My heart galloped faster than when I rode Apple.

"My aunt Eleanor wants us to go with her to the holiday party. Are you up for that?"

Despite how ill I was feeling, I had a sudden burst of energy, and if he weren't driving, I would've hopped over the console and kissed him. My excitement dried up when I thought about something he'd said. "You don't do parties."

He licked his lips. "I will for you."

Don't cry. Don't cry. But I couldn't help the excitement gripping me. Happy tears surfaced. I officially had a date for the party. More importantly, I had a boyfriend. *So cool. So not what I'd expected in my sophomore year of high school.* I couldn't wait to tell Momma. I couldn't wait to gush to Celia. But then Daddy came to mind, and my elation withered.

The sign for the farm store jutted out in the distance.

Within a minute, Maiken wheeled into the gravel lot and parked near the farm store. "But…"

My heart flew into my throat. If he said not to tell anyone, I would give him matching black eyes.

He shifted into park. "I would like to get your dad's approval first. He does know that I like you. So I don't think he'll say no."

My eyes opened a little wider. "He does? You talked to him about us?" Boy I would've liked to be a fly on the wall when they had that conversation.

"Kind of. He asked me if I liked you, and I told him I did. His response was, 'If you so much as hurt my daughter, I will take matters into my own hands.' That was the extent of our talk. But I just want to confirm he's okay. My dad taught Ethan and me to make sure we have the dad's approval when we started dating. I guess he didn't tell you."

Daddy didn't talk much about dating and boys, and if he'd mentioned anything to Momma about his talk with Maiken, she hadn't said a word.

"We'll ask him together," I said. I had to hear my dad's approval. That way, I could tell Carter that if he had issues, then he could talk to Daddy.

Although if I knew Carter, he wasn't going to jump on board that easily.

Chapter 28

Maiken

I hopped out of the car and hurried around to open Quinn's door. She gawked.

Dad had always made sure he was opening doors for Mom. But my gentlemanly manners vanished when a bell dinged behind me.

Mrs. Thompson ran out of the farm store. "What happened? What's wrong?"

Quinn's throat bobbed as she climbed out of the Suburban. Her skin looked pale, as though she were about to pass out.

I held out my hand to help her.

Smiling as though I were her world, she gave me her small hand. "I feel terrible, Momma."

Mrs. Thompson dove into mom action, feeling Quinn's forehead and face. "You're burning up. Let's get you inside."

I glanced down at the parking lot before going in. Only four trees lay on the ground, wrapped in wire. Liam had mentioned that they sometimes sold out of trees before Christmas. If that were the case, then I didn't have a job anymore. It was probably best anyway. I had to get my grades up, our first basketball game was a week away, and I had to get my head around playing point guard. The only downside to not working was money. I'd pocketed a couple of hundred dollars from the short time I'd worked, which would suffice for gifts.

The farm store was empty. Quinn sat on stool, a sheen of sweat coating her skin, while her mom inserted a thermometer in her mouth. Then Mrs. Thompson stuck a straw into a juice box. "Do your brothers know you left school?"

Quinn shook her head, shifting her attention to me.

Mrs. Thompson's brown eyes opened wide as she raked her gaze over my face. "What happened to your nose?"

I considered whether to tell her that Carter had punched me but quickly decided that our differences should be kept between us. Besides, she didn't need to hear how her son threw a mean punch.

Mr. Thompson emerged from the back room, wearing a ball cap, a tan jacket, and dirty jeans. "What's going on?" After he took one look at Quinn then me, that mean look he usually wore etched his strong jaw.

Mrs. Thompson went behind the counter. "Quinn has the flu."

He stabbed a finger at me. "Why do you have a black eye?"

"It's nothing. Brother stuff." I wasn't exactly lying, although that wasn't a way to start a relationship with my girlfriend's father.

The word *girlfriend* sounded foreign, but I was ready to have a girl. I was ready to build a relationship with Quinn.

"Was it that Stevens boy?" Mr. Thompson snarled. "Did he try something with Quinn?"

Quinn rolled her eyes.

I flinched back slightly, wondering why Mr. Thompson would think Chase would be foolish to do something to Quinn. Tessa and Quinn didn't like each other, so by default, maybe Mr. Thompson thought Chase would support his sister.

Quinn pulled the thermometer out of her mouth, waving at her father. "Daddy." Her voice was soft and sweet, reminding me of how my sisters could take away Dad's anger in a flash. "I'm not feeling well. Chase didn't do anything."

Mr. Thompson chewed on the inside of his cheek. He didn't look convinced.

Mrs. Thompson circled the counter with a first-aid kit in her hand. "Jeff, Chase is a good boy."

He arched a brow at his wife. "Debatable."

Interesting comments on both their parts. I had to side with Mr. Thompson.

"Quinn, put that thermometer back in," Mrs. Thompson said. "Maiken, sit on this stool next to Quinn."

I didn't move from my spot near the table of jams. "I'm fine." My nose wasn't bleeding anymore, but I could feel the tightness around it from the dried blood.

Quinn patted the stool. "Let Momma at least clean the blood before you go back to school." Her words were muffled as she talked around the thermometer.

That was a great idea. I didn't want to alarm Ethan.

Mr. Thompson watched me intently as though he were thinking hard about whether we were telling the truth.

Cleaning up the dried blood, Mrs. Thompson asked, "Is it broke?"

I wiggled it a little. "No, ma'am." Carter punched hard, but he hadn't broken it.

Mr. Thompson grabbed his keys from the counter. "I need to go into town, Hazel."

"Sir," I said. "I noticed you only have a few trees left."

"I'm glad you brought it up. We're pretty much sold out. So I'm sorry—I won't be needing you anymore."

I wasn't surprised. "If you do need a hand anywhere else, I'm available."

He nodded once. "I'll keep that in mind."

My pulse thrummed a fast tune as I asked, "Do I have your approval to date Quinn?" I held my breath and checked on Quinn. She seemed to be doing the same.

Mrs. Thompson beamed as she deposited the spent gauze pad into the trash.

Mr. Thompson studied his wife as though they were speaking telepathically. After a beat, he sighed. "Maiken, you should be asking my daughter, not me."

I released the air in my lungs. Ninety percent of me had known he would say yes based on the conversation we'd had, but that nagging voice in my head had still made me doubt.

Quinn squealed. "I said yes, Daddy."

Her dad grinned.

I felt compelled to respond. "I will be the perfect gentleman."

"We know you will," Mrs. Thompson added.

Quinn handed the thermometer to her mom and threw her arms around her dad. "You don't need to worry. It's time I date."

Growling under his breath, he smoothed a hand over her hair. "You grew up way too fast." He narrowed his eyes at me. "If you don't treat her like the lady she is, I will cut off more than your legs. Do you get my drift?"

Loud and clear.

I raised a hand. "My dad would be the first in line to set me straight if he were alive. You have my word, sir."

Quinn kissed her dad on the cheek.

Now it was time to take my girl to a party.

Chapter 29

Quinn

The stands in the gym were packed with kids, parents, and teachers from both Kensington High and Forest Grove High. The cheerleaders from both schools huddled on their respective side of the basketball court while both teams warmed up.

Celia and I were sandwiched in between Emma on my side and Ethan on Celia's side. Maiken's mom and Kade sat behind us. The other Maxwell kids were home with Eleanor and Martin, and the younger ones had come down with the flu, which seemed to be making the rounds with everyone. Even Carter and Liam had come down with the flu.

Celia nudged me before she whispered in my ear. "There's your boyfriend."

I got all tingly. It seemed odd to hear *your boyfriend*. I would've never in a million years thought I would have a boyfriend.

The team was warming up, and Maiken was shooting free throws from the three-point line, and every shot went in. Whispers peppered around us.

"Ooh, he's going to be great for the team," a dad in front of us said to his wife.

I still wasn't sure he should be a point guard. I'd seen Chase play, and he wasn't good at three-point shots. Regardless, Maiken looked especially handsome in his basketball uniform—tall, muscles toned, and his hair tamed. I couldn't wait to go out on dates with him.

Since he'd brought me home from school a week before, I'd been sick with the flu. I'd missed so much school that I was trying to get caught up on all the homework I'd missed.

"I hear you're going to the Stevenses' party with Maiken." Emma sounded sad.

"I thought you were going." When we'd been standing down at the lake, she'd all but demanded that Maiken go, and she'd given me the impression that she couldn't attend if Maiken didn't.

Her ponytail swung as she shook her head. "I'm not allowed to go." She stared out at the court. "Be careful. It is Tessa's turf."

"Do you know something I don't?" Surely Tessa wouldn't act out at her own party.

The squeak of the basketball shoes on the wood floor echoed in the gymnasium.

Emma's cheekbones sparkled from her pink blush. "She doesn't like that you're officially dating Maiken."

"How does she know that?" I hadn't said a word to anyone except Celia. I gave my best friend a sidelong glance.

"I didn't say anything," Celia said. "I swear on my grandmother's grave."

She loved her grandmother, so I tended to believe her. Besides, word was bound to get around school. I was just relieved that Maiken and me dating wasn't a rumor.

Regardless, I was sure Chase wasn't jumping up and down for joy over the news either. The conversation we'd had in the cafeteria skipped through my mind.

"Let me make it clear again. I like you, Quinn. I told you last night I wouldn't give up."

Now that I was dating Maiken, maybe Chase would stop paying attention to me.

"Is there anyone owning up to the rumor about Maiken and me having... you know?" I spoke low so Christine and Kade wouldn't hear me. I didn't think they would because they were chatting about Maiken playing point guard instead of shooting guard. I'd heard bits and pieces every now and again.

Emma frowned. "Dana told a friend that Maiken was unavailable, and somehow the rumor morphed into something completely different, or at least that was her answer."

The area around Celia's eyes crinkled as she regarded Emma. "And you thought it would be me. Thanks a lot."

Emma leaned over me slightly. "Celia, I'm sorry. But Dana is a nice girl. She was devastated when the rumor blew up. But we're in high school. Aren't we?"

I just wished I wasn't the brunt of the rumors.

A hand landed on my shoulder. "Quinn," Christine said. "Do you have a dress for the party?"

Celia, Emma, and I turned.

"Lacey has a few dresses that might fit you if you need one," Kade said.

"Mom," Emma said. "I want to go."

"We talked about this," Christine said. "Maybe next year will be your time."

"She can help my mom," Celia piped in.

"Isn't Liam helping?" I asked. The last I'd overheard Momma and Liam talking, he had said he was.

Celia shied away briefly. "He is. But we could always use more help."

Ethan had been super quiet, watching his brother. "I can help too," he added. "I want to see what all the hype over this party is."

"Both of you are not going," Christine said in a motherly voice. "Now I don't want to hear anymore about it."

Ethan and Emma huffed but said nothing more.

The entire gym quieted when Alex Baker's parents came in.

"What's going on?" Emma asked.

"Those are Alex's parents," I said.

"You mean the one who was a great basketball player?" Ethan asked.

"So he was the point guard that Maiken told me about," Christine said more than asked.

I cast a look over my shoulder at Christine. She seemed worried all of a sudden. Maiken had big shoes to fill, but I had no doubt he would be great.

After the Bakers found a seat, the conversations perked up again.

Both teams huddled around their coaches. The cheerleaders got into formation behind the basketball goals, the rival team on one end and Kensington on the other. Tessa Stevens stood out with her gold ribbon tied around her ponytail while the others, including our head cheerleader, wore royal-blue ribbons. It figured Tessa had to be different.

The color guard marched out to center court.

The first game of the basketball season was about to begin, and my nerves started to sing. I'd sat in the stands many times at basketball games, ogling Alex as he ran up and down the court. But now I was about to watch my boyfriend in his first game for Kensington High. I was nervous for him. I knew how important basketball was to Maiken, and for that, I wanted him to shine, not for me but for himself. I wanted the fans to love him like they'd loved Alex.

As if Maiken knew what I was thinking, he broke his attention from Coach Dean and glanced up at the stands. Whether he was seeking me out or his family, I smiled and waved, and when he grinned from ear to ear, my heart melted.

Chapter 30

Maiken

The ref blew the whistle. "Time-out!"

I ground my back teeth hard, glancing at the scoreboard. *Pathetic.* We were down by twenty with only five minutes left in the game.

The team gathered around Coach Dean, who had handed me my butt during halftime. Even still, I couldn't get my shit together. I didn't know what was happening with me. I couldn't pass. I couldn't shoot. I couldn't read my team, and as a point guard, I sucked.

Coach shot daggers at me. "What the heck are you doing out there, Maxwell? Have you ever played basketball?"

I was wondering the same thing. I was good. I was capable, yet the boos from the fans told me otherwise. Hell, the score said it all. Our opponents were good, but they'd had their own issues, missing several shots.

"I told you he was useless," Chase muttered.

I flared my nostrils so hard, I swore I had steam streaming out.

"Back off, Stevens," Liam snapped.

Chase's dirt-colored eyes became pinpoints.

Coach squatted down with his clipboard. "Can it, all of you, and listen up. Stevens, you don't belong under the basket. That's Thompson and Woods's job."

Hell yeah! Chase hadn't given me a chance to pass the ball to him, and anytime he caught a pass from Liam, Miller, or Woods, he couldn't convert the ball to a basket. It seemed to me that he hadn't played shooting guard at all. I was scratching my head as to why Coach thought Chase would be better than me at that position.

"Maxwell is ignoring me," Chase whined.

My upper lip twitched, but I tempered my anger for the moment. We were there to win a game. *Good luck with that when you can't even play the position.*

"Miller, you need to move more. Get around your opponent. And Maxwell, stop shooting the basketball every time you have the ball. You're a point guard now, and we're a team. Do you understand the concept of a team?"

Chase started to say something.

"One word, and I'll deck you right here," I said through gritted teeth.

Coach rose. "We're down by twenty. We can still come back. Now get out there. I want a zone defense. Maxwell, pass the damn ball."

I doubted we would win the game. I doubted Chase would listen to Coach. I doubted that I would be playing in the next game.

I got some water, willing the knots in my stomach to go away. They had taken up a home for the last several days. All week at school, I'd heard kids talking about the basketball game.

"Do you think Maxwell will be as good as Alex?" a boy had asked.

"I hear he's a god on the court," a girl had added.

"He can't be better than Alex Baker," another boy had said.

I had some big shoes to fill. I'd been up for the challenge until that conversation. I knew I was playing in a dead boy's position, but it really hadn't hit me until that week, so much so that I'd debated whether to back out of playing. But Coach had been stoked when he'd learned I would play point guard. He'd worked with me every day after practice, going over strategy and tactics with the position.

Moreover, I wasn't a quitter, no matter how bad things were, and I wasn't about to start.

The ref blew the whistle.

I finished the last of my water.

Liam slapped a hand on my back. "Ignore Chase's taunts, man. Play the game. I know you're good."

I appreciated his encouragement. Actually, it was something I needed to hear. Aside from the pressure of the first game, my new position, and knowing that the fans wanted Alex Baker back, I'd been feeling extremely melancholy that my dad wasn't there. Granted, he'd missed many of my games when he'd been on deployment, but I could always count on talking to him about the game when he called home.

I jogged up to the sideline to inbound the ball.

Miller, the shortest of the boys on the team and a small forward who was quick on his feet, was closest to me while the rest of the players darted in around each other.

I stole a quick look at the home side of the gym and zeroed in on one girl with butterscotch hair. Like she'd done earlier, she gave me the biggest smile, as though telling me I was doing great. My heart accelerated even more when I swung my gaze to my mom, who was sitting behind Quinn. She seemed so proud, giving me one of her megawatt smiles. They shouldn't be proud of me.

Thankfully, the ref blew the whistle before handing me the ball.

Get your head in the game. You know what to do. You know how the game is played. So what if you're not a shooting guard.

I blew out a breath, waving my hand at Chase to get around the big redhead who was manning him. Liam was trying to ditch his opponent. The only open person was Woods. He was as tall as Liam and primed to shoot the basket with a toss of his hands.

Just as I was about to throw the ball to Woods, one of the Forest Grove members slid in front of him.

Miller ran up, hands out, and I passed the ball to him. He then passed the ball to Liam, who spun around, and with one step, he went in for a layup and scored.

Finally.

My team ran down to get into our zone position. We'd been playing man-to-man defense, but that wasn't working. All of us seemed to have glue on the bottom of our basketball shoes.

"At least we know we can score when Maxwell doesn't have the ball," Chase murmured rather loudly behind me. "I think Maxwell's head is clouded over from all that sex he's having."

Ignore him. Ignore him. Ignore him. My problem was that when it came to Chase, I was finding it impossible to walk away.

"Careful, Stevens." Liam's tone could cut stone. "You're talking about my sister, and I don't care that we're in the middle of a game; I will knock you on your ass."

I wanted nothing more than to sew Chase's lips together so I would never hear his grating voice again.

Forest Grove was in position as their point guard, a short and lean boy, carried the ball down the court. He held up three fingers, signaling to his team the play he wanted to set up. Coach had taught me a few signals to let our men know what I wanted them to do. That night, signals hadn't worked, mainly because Chase wouldn't acknowledge me.

The Forest Grove man barely reached the top of the key when he shot the ball.

Swish was all I heard before boos filled the gymnasium, drowning out the cheering of the Forest Grove fans.

Then a Kensington High fan shouted, "You suck, Maxwell. Get off the court."

Chase laughed.

All sound died, and red as bright as the sun on a hot summer day blinded me. I stalked over to Chase and threw a punch right to his jaw. Chase lunged, tackling me to the hardwood, ramming his fists into my face once then twice before someone pulled him off me.

Liam extended his hand as all the players on both teams made a circle around me. The refs pushed their way in. The coaches were right on their heels.

Blood dripped from my nose for the second time in a week.

Chase bared his teeth.

Coach Dean mashed his lips into the thinnest line I'd ever seen. "Both of you are done for the night. Sit your asses on the bench. Both of you."

The gym was so quiet, we could hear a pin drop. I kept my head down, afraid if I looked at my mom, I would lose it again, not because I was sad, but because she would have disappointment written all over her.

Chase stomped over to the bench and threw his head in his hands.

I couldn't sit idle or among the crowd or next to Chase. I needed air, or I needed to stick my head in a locker and bang the door against my skull a few times.

With the blood pumping through me at breakneck speeds, I grabbed a towel and left the gym. No sooner had the zero temperature hit my bare arms and legs than the sweat on my body froze, a welcome relief for the moment. I paced the courtyard behind the sports complex, holding the towel to my nose. I would have two black eyes, although the one Carter had given me was yellowing.

"Bro." Ethan's voice carried on the wind. "What is going on with you?"

I continued to pace, seething and berating myself. "Fuck if I know."

"Do you want my two cents?"

I clutched the towel, finally coming to a halt inches from him. I always gave him advice when he asked or I offered. "I'm listening." I would do anything to help get past whatever it was that was bringing me down and causing me to play like an amateur.

"No one can expect you to be the dead boy."

I laughed, but it wasn't light or funny. "Tell that to the crowd."

"Since when do you worry over the crowd? You're always in your element on the court. What's changed?"

"Filling his shoes is eating me inside."

A spotlight from high above on the building shined down, giving Ethan a glow as if he were an angel. "Why?"

As I considered my brother, something surreal came to me, and in that moment, I was looking into the eyes of my father as if he were standing there. "Everyone has been talking about Alex Baker, and the fact that he's dead somehow gets me thinking about Dad."

"Maybe that's the problem," Ethan said. "You haven't processed Dad's death."

I was sure I hadn't. "And you have?" It would take years. Or maybe never.

I headed for the sports complex. The air was starting to seep into my bones.

Ethan walked alongside me. "Not in the least. But you have to find a way to focus on the court. Why don't you ask Coach to play one game as shooting guard? He's really never seen you in action in a game. And don't say he has in practice. We both know practice isn't a game."

I'd played better during practice.

Heat blanketed me as soon as I was inside, but I shivered none-theless.

"Stevens is horrible at shooting guard," Ethan continued. "He doesn't move around. He can't shoot. And he seems to stay near the net. What's that all about?"

I wasn't in the mood to figure out the answers. Besides, all I could come up with was that I was the problem, not Chase.

Footsteps resonated in the empty hall before I spied Quinn. She was a sight for sore eyes.

"I'll let Mom know you're okay," Ethan said before his backside faded down the hall.

Mom wasn't going to be happy with me, and no doubt she would scold me when I got home. But right then, that didn't matter. What did matter was seeing Quinn. I hadn't seen her since I'd asked her to go out with me. That was a week ago, although it felt longer than that.

She craned her neck to look up at me. "Are you okay? I looked for you in the locker room. I thought you and Chase had killed each other."

We still might. "The game over?"

She nodded, staring at me with so many questions stamped in her eyes.

"I would like to spend time with you now that you're feeling better," I said. "But Coach will want to talk to me tonight, and then my mom will probably ground me." The latter was a given.

"We have school tomorrow, and I have a load of homework to catch up on anyway. I just wanted to make sure you were okay." Sadness hung on the last three words.

I lowered my head until our lips were almost touching. "Now that you're here, I'm good." Then I kissed her—no tongue action, just a soft and tender kiss. "I can't wait to take you to the party."

A laugh broke out in my head. I was the last person interested in that party, but for her, I was finding that I would do anything, especially when it made her light up like a bright star.

Chapter 31

Quinn

O*h my God. The party's tonight.* I literally had to catch my breath several times during the day, and it wasn't only due to the holiday gala, but I had my first ever date. I'd hoped to spend time with Maiken during the last week, but that hadn't happened. His mom had grounded him, and since Daddy didn't have any more trees to sell, Maiken wasn't working at the farm. Plus, I hardly saw him at school.

The only time I'd gotten to talk to him was at a recent basketball game. Coach had benched him for starting that fight with Chase. Maiken couldn't play again until after the holidays.

He'd said he expected to be punished, but that was the extent of that topic and sadly the extent of our conversation with the exception of the party. At first, I'd thought he would cancel on me since he'd been punished. But his mom had given him the green light thanks in part to Eleanor. She'd said it would be good for Maiken to get out and clear his head.

Knuckles rapped on my bedroom door before it opened. "Quinn," Carter said.

I had fifteen minutes before Maiken picked me up, and the last thing I wanted to do was argue with my brother. I was in a good mood, and I didn't want anything to spoil my night. Regardless, I'd avoided the subject of boys and dating and even Maiken with Carter.

I brushed my hair in front of the mirror over my white dresser. Mom wanted me to pin up my hair, but I wanted to leave it down. I liked the way the ends were curled and how my hair framed my face. "I'm not speaking to you."

He sat on the edge of my twin bed.

My room was the smallest bedroom out of the four in our two-story farmhouse. While we had acres and acres of land, our house appeared like a tiny dot amid all the rolling hills. Even our barn was almost bigger than our house.

"You're not going to like what I have to say, then."

I spun around on my bare feet. "What's wrong?" He'd better not say he hurt Maiken again. I would scream if he so much as interfered in my first ever relationship.

Carter combed his fingers through his messy brown hair. "Stay home. Don't go to the Stevenses'."

I planted my hands on my hips. "I got Daddy's approval to date. So butt out."

"It's got nothing to do with Maxwell," he said with an easy expression. "And I know Dad gave his blessing."

"If you're about to tell me you heard a rumor, then leave. I'm tired of the word 'rumor' and the meaning of it."

Carter clasped his hands in his lap. "I haven't heard anything. Call this a gut feeling. You're going to Tessa's house. She hates you. Chase has no love for Maxwell."

"His name is Maiken." I bit my tongue.

"It's not a place for you. Max-Maiken will only get you into trouble. I don't want to see you get hurt."

I sat down beside him, my chest warming at how much I loved my brother despite his flaws. "I know you worry about me. Thank you for being a big brother. But I can handle myself. I've been tormented by Tessa for so long that I think I'm becoming immune to her anyway." That wasn't exactly true, but I had been a little bolder lately. Case in point was at the skating rink when I'd pushed Tessa and given her the middle finger. I would've never even spoken to her the way I had at school that morning when she'd confronted me about her party. "I like Maiken. He's a gentleman and nice guy."

A muscle ticked in Carter's jaw as he moved some of my hair behind my ear. "You know I will kill him if he breaks your heart."

I grinned, knowing full well what my brother was capable of. "Trust in me. I know someday I'll get my heart broken, but isn't that all part of growing up? Haven't you had a girl break your heart?" I didn't know of any. In fact, Carter hadn't had a steady girlfriend that I knew of.

His lips curled into a devilish smile. "My love life is not part of this discussion."

I tilted my head. "And neither is mine."

He pushed to his feet. "Be careful tonight."

I nodded as he strutted out. Grown-ups would be there, so I couldn't imagine anything awful happening.

Momma came in while I slipped on my heels. She'd bought me a very simple toned-down gold dress with a rounded neckline that dipped to the tops of my breasts. The sparkles in it brought out my light-brown hair and eyes.

She placed a hand on her chest. "You look beautiful."

My cheeks flushed. "Do you think Maiken will think so?"

She rolled her eyes. "Any boy would be blind not to notice. Come on. Your ride is here."

My pulse fired at warp speed. Suddenly, I felt sick.

Momma noticed as she untied her apron. She always wore one when working in the kitchen. "No need for nerves. He'll adore you."

Part of my nerves was a result of my thoughts wandering over what Carter had said. Why I was thinking something could go wrong was beyond me.

But that eerie feeling settled in the pit of my stomach.

Chapter 32

Maiken

The Stevenses' house was bigger than my aunt and uncle's estate. A winding staircase curled up to the top floor. A crystal chandelier hung as the centerpiece, illuminating the white-tiled foyer. Red flowers decorated the large tables and were tucked in and around chairs and a loveseat.

Men dressed in tuxedos or sharp suits and women in colorful, sparkly jewelry and dresses milled about with glasses of what looked to be champagne. Christmas music played from somewhere overhead, and waiters and waitresses served trays of bubbly and tiny finger foods.

"This reminds me of a scene out of *Gone with the Wind*," Quinn cooed.

Emma would be sighing left and right if she were there. She loved parties and *Gone with the Wind*. Personally, I didn't see the draw of a house full of people talking and laughing. *Stuffy, rich people.* I wasn't dissing on rich people. After all, my aunt and uncle had money. But I was standing in the house of my enemy, and that was the main reason I had a bad taste in my mouth. I almost backed out. I didn't want to see Chase or run the chance of finishing the fight we'd started on the court.

Speaking of the court, Coach had benched me for three games. He'd been so angry with me that I was surprised he hadn't passed out from all the screaming he'd done in his office after that game. However, he hadn't suspended Chase.

"You were the one to throw the first punch," Coach had said. "Not only that, we need to work harder at sharpening your skills as a point guard."

But that night wasn't about basketball or me. I was there because of the pretty girl holding my hand as if she were holding on for her life— afraid she might drown if she let go. That same girl had rendered me speechless when I'd picked her up earlier that night.

One look at her, and my body had gone haywire. Her legs went on forever under a gold dress that hugged her curves. She wasn't exactly a tall girl, but the heels she was wearing made her legs seem long, and to my chagrin, I'd been tongue-tied and unable to speak. The car ride over had been quiet. She hadn't uttered a peep either.

Liam emerged around a group of old people. He looked dapper in his black pants and white button-up shirt. "Care for a drink?"

"Liam," Quinn said. "We're underage."

"Chill, sis. It's ginger ale. No booze at this party. I guess there's a silent auction going on, and the proceeds go to Mothers Against Drunk Driving. The Stevenses are trying to help out the Bakers."

I snagged a glass—anything to get rid of the sand in my throat and get my tongue to work.

Liam kissed Quinn on the cheek. "You look pretty." Then his hard gaze landed on me like a bullet to the chest. "Dude, hand-holding with my sister. Nothing more."

I instantly felt my face burn like molten lava because I'd already been having unclean thoughts about Quinn and me. I couldn't get the image out of my head of her sitting on my lap as we'd kissed that day in the funhouse.

Think basketball. Think anything but kissing Quinn.

I chugged the ginger ale then replaced the empty glass on Liam's tray.

Quinn dug her nails into my palm. "Liam, don't embarrass me."

He shrugged as he moved on to other guests.

Quinn and I stepped deeper into the house.

"Don't leave my side," she said softly.

"I'll try not to." I honestly didn't know what we would do for two or three hours.

Grown-ups were everywhere. Aside from Liam, I didn't see anyone from school, including Chase or Tessa. I knew Celia was there, working for her.

We weaved in and out of guests in a vast living room that spilled out to the backyard through the open French doors. Heaters stood tall around the large brick patio with more people clustered around them, no doubt trying to keep warm.

It seemed weird to me that people would stand out in the freezing temps with drinks in their hands.

"Is y-your m-mom still mad about your suspension?" Quinn asked.

We found an open spot outside a library where we could stop and talk.

"Mad isn't the word," I said, scanning the room and on high alert for my enemy.

She shivered. "H-have you t-talked to Chase at all since then?" I couldn't tell if her stuttering was because she was cold, nervous, or both.

We had taken off our coats when we arrived and given them to a butler. So I took off my suit jacket and draped it around her shoulders. It was the first time I'd worn a suit since my dad's funeral.

She beamed up at me, and thoughts of my dad waned as I locked eyes with a girl whose smile said so much—*I want you, I like you,* and *we should get out of here.* I was getting the feeling that she would rather show me how to feed a horse than stand at a party where I believed we didn't belong.

"Let's make a deal," I said. "No talk of Chase or his sister."

She nodded in quick succession as she nudged me.

Any notion of avoiding Chase vanished as he came toward us.

Great. Hold it together, Maxwell. Don't make a fool of yourself.

His swagger was irritating as was the cheeky grin plastered on his face.

Quinn's hand was cemented to mine.

Chase sneered. "I see you have the balls to show your face in my house." Then he set his attention on Quinn, erasing any signs that he hated me. "You look beautiful."

Her cheeks reddened. "Th-thank you."

"You're adorable when you stutter," he said.

I rolled my eyes. "Let's go, Quinn."

He unbuttoned his tuxedo jacket. Yeah, he was all decked out in a tux. His hair was slicked back, and his pimples were camouflaged with makeup. I could tell because Emma often did the same thing. Quinn had masked her black eyes with makeup too. I hadn't bothered to cover up my black eyes. Luckily, they weren't as dark as I'd thought they would be.

Chase held out his hand to Quinn. "Would you dance with me?"

She reared back. "Did you know th-that in 1518, dozens of p-people died from dancing?"

Chase choked out a laugh. "For real?"

I squeezed Quinn's hand, trying to tell her to calm down. "She's my date, man. So back off." I didn't want to answer for her. I didn't want to come off as possessive as her brother, but I could feel her tension.

Besides, I didn't see people dancing anywhere in the immediate vicinity. I did, however, lock eyes with Kade. He was clean-shaven, standing tall in a tux next to his wife, who was chatting with my aunt Eleanor. Kade inclined his head then faintly moved it as though telling me not to cause a scene.

As much as I wanted to finish what I'd started on the court, I'd promised my mom that I would be on my best behavior. So I nodded at Kade, hoping he would get the message that I wasn't about to start trouble.

Yet he still made his way over. "Everything okay, boys?"

Chase extended his hand to Kade. "Nice to see you." He sounded as though he knew Kade well.

Kade shook his hand. "It's been a while. How's the jaw?"

If I weren't mistaken, Kade was provoking Chase.

"Better than his black eye," Chase said. "So, Quinn, about that dance?"

She looked to me for an answer.

Holy cow! She was considering dancing with the jerk.

Or so I thought until she said, "M-Maiken is m-my date."

Chase gave her a sweet smirk. "It's just a dance. I promise you won't die from dancing."

As if she had an epiphany of sorts, she dipped her head. "O-one dance."

I felt the air leaving my lungs. Quinn's acceptance jabbed my gut as if she'd taken a knife and stabbed me with it.

Chase puffed out his chest and held out his elbow.

Quinn lifted up on her toes and kissed me on the cheek. "I'll b-be right back." Then she hooked her arm around Chase's.

I wasn't going to stand there and let him have his way. He wasn't getting the girl. It was bad enough he'd kept his position as shooting guard and hadn't gotten benched.

But Quinn had made her decision. It was only a dance.

Like hell. Their bodies would be pressed together.

I took one step to follow them when Kade stopped me. "No, man. I get it. If I were in your shoes right now, I would go ape shit. Actually, I did when a guy touched Lacey. But I wasn't at a party with adults. I'm sure Quinn said yes so you two wouldn't throw down. Why don't you ask Lacey or my mom to dance? That way, you can keep an eye on Quinn."

I didn't dance and never had. I wasn't sure I ever would.

But when Chase tossed an amused, condescending look over his shoulder, dancing wasn't what I had in mind.

Chapter 33

Quinn

I held on to Chase for dear life. If I didn't, I would probably fall. I hadn't wanted to say yes, but I didn't want a fight to break out. The tension between Maiken and Chase had only grown tighter and tighter, and a party with adults wasn't the place for them to air out their differences. I hoped Maiken would understand. I'd wanted to tell him my reasoning but not in front of Chase.

But you're leading Chase on.

I would tell Chase my feelings when we were on the dance floor, wherever that was. Then a crazy thought slammed into me. What if Chase was leading me into the lion's den? What if he was bringing me to Tessa? She hadn't been in my face or gone out of her way to pick on me, which I thought for sure she would have when she'd learned that Maiken and I were dating. Maybe the last week had just been the calm before the storm. She was probably planning her attack for that night.

Chase lowered his head until his breath brushed the shell of my ear. "You're beautiful." He sounded as though he truly meant it.

"It's o-only one dance. N-nothing more."

His lips curled into a devilish smile, one that sent a bad shiver up my arms.

As we passed Lacey and Eleanor, Lacey stopped us, holding on to her champagne glass. "Quinn, I love your dress." Her big green eyes swept over me as she opened Maiken's suit jacket that was still draped over me.

I let go of Chase's arm, thankful Lacey had distracted us. "Thank you." I sighed, feeling relieved that I hadn't stuttered.

"Where's my nephew?" Eleanor asked in an even tone. She was as pretty as her daughter-in-law. Both had their hair swept up in a fancy hairstyle, and Lacey wore a black halter dress that hung to just above her knees. Eleanor wore a deep-blue tea-length dress.

Chase stiffened.

"He's near the library, talking to Kade." I started to ask where Martin was, but a petite girl serving the last of the shrimp to a group of adults next to us laughed.

I knew that laugh. I turned and tapped Celia on the shoulder.

Finally, someone could give me a pep talk and erase the anxiety that had settled in my stomach. Honestly, I'd been a bag of nerves since my conversation with Carter. At first, I hadn't thought Tessa would do something stupid. Yet now that I was at her house, among her family, and in the presence of her brother, I didn't want to be there. I didn't belong amid the rich, and the party was mostly adults whom I didn't know.

I should ask Maiken to take me home. We could spend our night up in the loft of the barn, talking or maybe kissing. That sounded so much better to me.

Celia's eyes nearly popped out of her head when she noticed Chase. "I don't understand. Liam said Maiken was here."

"I am." Maiken's voice wrapped around me like a heavy blanket on a cold, cold night—warm, cozy, and loving.

I pivoted on my heel, ready to throw my arms around my boyfriend when I stumbled.

Chase and Maiken caught me at the same time. Maiken growled, spitting fire at Chase.

Once I was steady, I took in a quiet breath. I was suddenly feeling claustrophobic. "Excuse me. I need to use the bathroom."

"I'll show you where it is," Celia said, coming to my rescue.

"I'll take her," Chase offered. "It's my house. I know where it is."

"I do too," Celia returned mockingly.

Maiken's gaze was glued to Chase. "I'll come with."

I pressed a hand to his chest. "No. I-I'll be right back." Before Chase or Maiken could protest, I darted through the crowd on wobbly legs.

"I'm right behind you," Celia said. "Keep going straight, and at the archway, bank right."

But instead of following her instructions, I veered left. The patio doors were open and inviting as the mixture of hot and cold mingled together and breezed over me. At that point, I didn't care how cold it was outside. I needed fresh air.

A twenty-something couple on the patio held drinks and chatted underneath heaters.

"Where are you going?" Celia asked.

Far away. I was stupid for getting so excited over a party.

A fire flickered out of a stone pit adjacent to the pool. I eased down onto one of the four curved benches that had flannel blankets covering them.

Celia cozied up to me. "You look scared. Did Tessa find you?"

I rubbed my hands together near the fire. "I haven't seen her. I just needed air. Chase asked me to dance, and instead of saying no, I said yes so Chase and Maiken wouldn't fight. But I really don't want to be here."

"The party isn't all that great. But you're on a date with Maiken. Aren't you happy about that?"

"It doesn't feel like a date. I shouldn't have come. I shouldn't have made such a big deal about a stupid party. I'd rather be somewhere else with Maiken."

"Then tell him. He does look like he's suffocating."

Or ready to do something drastic to Chase.

"Celia," a lady called before she glanced down and saw me. "Oh, Quinn."

I stood. "Mrs. Corbett, it's so nice to see you." I gave Celia's mom a hug. It had been a while since I'd seen an older replica of Celia. Mother and daughter looked exactly alike. They each had a button nose and espresso eyes and hair. Both wore glasses, and the only difference was that Mrs. Corbett was older.

"You look especially pretty tonight," Mrs. Corbett cooed. "Are you having a good time?"

I shrugged.

Celia rose. "It's an adult party, Mom. Not much fun to be had here."

Mrs. Corbett wrapped her arms around herself. "Celia, I need you to keep serving food."

Celia frowned. "See me before you go, Quinn."

I nodded. "I should get back to Maiken." Maybe Chase had left. Maybe he'd forgotten about the dance.

Celia waved as she followed her mom back into the house.

For a beat, I warmed my hands over the fire, noticing how the backyard was decorated much like the inside of the house. Poinsettias dotted the edge of the patio where the stone pavement met the brownish-green grass that still held remnants of snow. The trees rimming the property twinkled from the white string lights. Glowing candles floated on the pool's surface. The sky was clear. The stars were out. The moon was full and bright.

Suddenly, I knew the perfect place to take Maiken.

I skirted a bench when Tessa's laugh switched on the alarm in my head. *So much for avoiding her.*

"Quinn." Tessa said my name in a sweet but salty tone. "I've been looking for you."

Be nice. I didn't know what else to do other than to run like I usually did when I saw her. Yet running in heels wouldn't get me far.

She approached me, wearing a bright-red gown with a short-cropped sweater. Her black hair was braided, and if she didn't have maliciousness flickering in her eyes, then her beauty would shine.

I glanced over her shoulder. The twenty-something couple was still talking as they hovered under the heater.

"Don't worry," Tessa said. "I only want to talk."

I got the feeling she wanted to do more than talk. I mean, Tessa wasn't nice to me ever. But maybe she was changing her tune since it was Christmas.

"I heard you might skate again."

I'd never said such a thing to anyone. I might've thought about it, but I hadn't verbalized it at all.

"W-who told you that?"

"No one. I overheard Kade talking to his wife inside."

Kade had suggested that I compete. He probably said something like that, and Tessa took it out of context.

She crossed her arms over her chest, hunching into herself. "Well?"

"You heard wrong." Even if I were, I wouldn't tell her. She would drum up ways to make sure I didn't skate.

"You wouldn't beat me anyway." Her tone now had more salt than sugar.

I clamped down on my tongue. I wanted to beat Tessa at something. I wanted to show her that I was better than her.

That's not who you are.

My nostrils widened.

She smirked as though she could see my anger brewing. "Well, you wouldn't."

I inhaled deeply before pushing out all the air in my lungs. "It seems I already won."

She invaded my personal space. "Yeah. How's that?"

I edged back, studying her as my stomach tumbled with nausea. *Don't be afraid of her. She can't do anything to you at her party. Be bold and strong like your brothers.*

Carter wouldn't stand for her jeers at all, and neither would Liam. I often questioned why I hadn't inherited their confidence or, as Granny would say, their sass.

Nevertheless, it wasn't the place to get into an argument. I tried to get around her.

She blocked me. "Answer me."

I moved to my left.

She followed. "What are you? Mute?"

My hands began to shake as I curled my fingers into my palm. "I don't want to argue."

She rolled back her shoulders. "Answer me. How have you already won?"

I held on to my bottom lip. I couldn't get past her without hopping over a bench or falling into the pool unless I took the path around in the other direction. I gave her one last glare then started to turn when she grasped my arm to the point of pain.

"We're not done."

I tried to shrug her off, but she tightened her grip.

I wiggled my arm hard, but that only caused me to sway to one side, so much so that I could feel myself about to fall.

Her eyes opened wide.

My heart was in my throat. I silently pleaded with her not to let go because if she did, I was going into the icy water.

Then a cruel smile spread across her face.

If I was going in, then so was she.

As if in slow motion, her grip loosened. I gulped in air as I reached for her. When my fingers grazed the hem of her sweater, I latched on.

She squealed.

I screamed as I pulled her with me.

Chapter 34

Maiken

I waited for Quinn outside the bathroom, but when the door opened, a man with salt-and-pepper hair waltzed out. Panic surged through me. Just the same, I checked the bathroom, knowing she wasn't in there.

I also knew she wasn't with Chase. I'd left him with Lacey and Aunt Eleanor. He seemed to be entranced with Lacey and her baseball career.

I wandered around the house, searching for Quinn, when I saw Celia chatting with Liam in the kitchen.

I ponied up to the long island. "Hey, where's Quinn?"

Liam went as white as the marble on the countertop. It was as if he knew Quinn might be in trouble.

Celia wrinkled her nose. "I thought she was with you."

I didn't get a chance to talk or think when a chilling scream made the hairs on my arms stiffen. I sprinted out of the kitchen.

A group of guests were piling out onto the patio.

I pushed through them just as Tessa was falling into the pool on top of Quinn, who was sinking to the bottom.

I dove into the pool as if I were swimming in a fifty-meter race. In seconds, I was wrapping my arms around her. When I reached the surface, Quinn coughed, shivering.

Liam stood on the edge with his arms out. "Give her to me."

Celia stood next to him with her hand clamped over her mouth.

Quinn continued to cough as her teeth knocked together.

"What is going on?" a man asked. "Tessa?" His voice sounded strained as he helped Tessa out of the pool.

"Nothing, Daddy," Tessa said to the salt-and-pepper-haired man I'd bumped into outside the bathroom.

Mr. Stevens's tone dropped an octave. "Doesn't look like nothing."

I gripped Quinn's waist, lifting her up to Liam. "Take her over to the fire."

"There's blankets on the bench," Celia said. "Help Maiken out. I'll take Quinn."

"Get some towels," someone shouted.

We were going to need more than towels.

As Liam helped me out, Tessa sent a scathing look my way. "It's your girlfriend's fault."

It was good to know she acknowledged Quinn was my girl. Maybe that meant she would finally leave me alone.

Mr. Stevens ushered his daughter inside as the crowd went back to their normal conversations as if someone falling into a freezing pool happened all the time.

I hurried over to Quinn, feeling the sting of the cold seeping into my veins.

Quinn held on to the flannel blanket as she stared down at the fire. Her lips were blue, and her body quivered. "Cold."

Liam tossed me a blanket.

"I don't need one," I said.

"We need to get you out of those wet clothes, Quinn," Celia said.

She let out a weird laugh.

A low growl erupted from Liam.

I rolled my eyes, as did Celia.

Aunt Eleanor and Uncle Martin came out with expressions that were equal parts shock and concern.

"Oh my," Aunt Eleanor said.

Uncle Martin snapped into doctor mode. "Both of you need to get inside."

I would agree that the fire was only helping to thaw the ice from my body.

"What happened?" Aunt Eleanor asked.

"Yeah," Liam parroted.

Quinn shivered endlessly.

At that moment, it didn't matter what had happened. Quinn needed warmth. I was about to cocoon her in between my arms when Chase appeared.

Horror colored his ugly mug. "Please tell me my sister didn't throw you into the pool."

"Chase," Aunt Eleanor said. "Maybe you can get some dry clothes of Tessa's."

He nodded without squabbling. "You'll need some too, Maxwell. Come on. I'll take you both upstairs."

I didn't have time to be shocked over how nice Chase was acting.

Celia must have sensed Quinn's tension. "I'll come with."

Aunt Eleanor nodded. "That's a good idea."

"Maiken, after that, take Quinn home," Uncle Martin said.

We left my aunt and uncle standing by the fire as we followed Chase inside and up to the second floor.

"Celia, Tessa's room is down the hall on the left," Chase said. "Take Quinn into her bathroom." He opened the door to his bedroom. "Maxwell, in here."

"I'd rather stay with Quinn," I said.

"No," Chase and Liam said at the same time.

It wasn't as if I were going to watch her undress. I just wanted to make sure Tessa wasn't in there. "Where's Tessa?"

"She in my parents' room downstairs," Chase said.

Quinn had been quiet up until that moment. "I'll m-m-meet y-you right back h-h-here." Her teeth chattered.

It was then that I started to shiver. The sooner we both got out of the wet clothes, the faster we could warm up and the faster Quinn and I could get the hell out of the Stevenses' house. *My first party and my last one.* I vowed that I would stay away from parties, especially ones hosted by my enemy.

Chase disappeared into his room while I watched Celia and Quinn go into Tessa's. Then Chase threw a pair of sweatpants and a sweatshirt at me. "Bathroom is inside. I'll wait out here."

I walked into my enemy's lair, and my jaw came unhinged. The bedroom was bigger than my house in North Carolina. But I didn't linger to admire the black-and-white room. I made quick work of changing into dry clothes. Once I was done, I returned to find Chase was gone.

Liam was leaning against the wall. "Where are your clothes?"

"In his shower. I'll get them later." Or Chase could burn them. Mom wouldn't be happy since that was my only set of dress clothes, although Quinn had my suit jacket.

But my clothes weren't my concern. I went down to Tessa's bedroom and knocked.

"We'll be right out," Celia said in an elevated voice.

"So how's Carter?" I asked Liam. "Is he still pissed about that rumor?" I hadn't seen or talked to Carter since he'd punched me.

"He's fine. He's more protective than I am."

"You don't say," I teased.

He took off his bow tie. "Quinn is our baby sister. We've protected her since forever. So cut him some slack. Anyway, you have sisters. You'll see."

I couldn't protest. I would probably be in Carter's position one day, either with Emma, Charlotte, or Maple.

"Now, are you going to work on your point-guard skills?" Liam asked. "We need to win games."

Sadly, we'd lost our first two. At least I could say the second game wasn't my fault. "During Christmas break." We were out of school for two weeks. I would use that time to work hard at perfecting the position when I wasn't spending time with Quinn.

Tessa appeared at the end of the hall, wearing a terrycloth robe and a towel bundled around her head. She swung her dark gaze from Liam to me. Then without a word, she hoofed down to her room. Just as she was about to go in, Quinn came out.

Liam and I exchanged a hesitant look.

"You were in my room?" Tessa sounded outraged. "Ew! You're in my clothes? Who said you could wear my clothes?"

Quinn bumped Tessa's shoulder with her own as she passed. "I'll return them."

"Don't bother," Tessa said.

"What happened anyway?" I asked as the two girls swapped venom.

Quinn held her head high. "Accident." She started walking toward me then paused. "Oh, and Tessa. You know that rhyme you blab about me all the time? How does it go? Quinn, Quinn never wins. I'll never get the boy."

Tessa rolled her eyes. "So?"

The tension bounced off the walls.

Celia scooted around Tessa to stand beside Liam.

Quinn took my hand. "I did get the boy." Then she tugged on my arm. The four of us headed to the staircase.

After hearing that, I had no words. Tessa was a piece of work for sure.

"Quinn," Tessa called. "You haven't won anyone or anything yet."

Quinn let go of me then spun on her heel. "When school starts back up after the holidays, be prepared for a different Quinn."

My eyebrows flew to my hairline as I glanced at Liam, whose mouth hung open.

I didn't know what my girlfriend meant by a *different Quinn*, but I was eager yet wary to find out.

DEAR READER

I hope you enjoyed reading about all the new Maxwells. There are more books in the series on the horizon. Books 2 and 3 will feature more of Maiken and Quinn. If you would like to stay up-to-date on Maxwell news, come join my reader group on Facebook: https://www.facebook.com/groups/maxwellmania/

When you have a moment, I would super appreciate a quick review. It doesn't have to be long, but would love for you to share your excitement about My Heart to Touch. You can leave a review on Amazon, Goodreads or Bookbub . Links to these platforms can be found on the next page.

DON'T MISS OUT

Stay up-to-date on sales and new releases. I post frequent updates in my reader group on Facebook. You can join here: Maxwell Mania: https://www.facebook.com/groups/maxwellmania/
Follow me on any of the platforms below or signup for my newsletter at http://sbalexander.com/newsletter or visit my website at http://sbalexander.com

f facebook.com/sbalexander.authorpage

y twitter.com/sbalex_author

◎ instagram.com/sbalexanderauthor

a amazon.com/author/sbalexander

BB bookbub.com/authors/s-b-alexander

g goodreads.com/sbalexander

ALSO BY S.B. ALEXANDER

To read samples and find out where to purchase all books visit: http://sbalexander.com.

The Maxwell Family Saga:

My Heart to Touch - Book 1

My Heart to Hold – Book 2 (releasing 2019)

My Heart to Keep – Book 3 (releasing 2019)

The Maxwell Series:

Dare to Kiss - Book 1

Dare to Dream – Book 2

Dare to Love – Book 3

Dare to Dance - Book 4

Dare to Live - Book 5

Dare to Breathe - Book 6

The Maxwell Series Boxed Set – Books 1-3

Dare to Kiss Coloring Book Companion

The Vampire SEAL Series:

On the Edge of Humanity – Book 1

On the Edge of Eternity – Book 2

On the Edge of Destiny – Book 3

On the Edge of Misery - Book 4

On the Edge of Infinity - Book 5

The Vampire SEAL Collection - Boxed Set

Stand Alone Books

Breaking Rules

Rescuing Riley

The Hart Series:

Hart of Darkness

Hart of Vengeance - Coming Soon

Hart of Redemption - Coming Soon

ACKNOWLEDGMENTS

Writing and publishing a book takes a village. But I couldn't be more thankful to the one person who gives me the inspiration to do what I love—my husband. He's been such a guiding light as he battles one of the worse diseases with no cure. He fills my heart with so much joy. He always has a smile on his face, he's always laughing, and he's always making sure I'm taken care of. He's my angel. I couldn't do this without him.

I'm also grateful to the team behind me who helps me every step of the way from my editor, RedAdept Editing, my beta readers, my ARC team, my cover designer, Hang Le, my assistant, Alexandra Amor, and everyone in Maxwell Mania. Thank you, thank you, thank you!

A big hug and mad love for Heather Carver for keeping me focused and motivating me everyday to write, and to Kylie Sharp for always being a phone call away. Love you gals.

Finally, to all the readers and bloggers around the world, thank you for taking a chance on me.